SCARDUST

Suzanne
van Rooyen

Entangled Publishing, LLC
2614 South Timberline Road
Suite 109
Fort Collins, CO 80525
Visit our website at www.entangledpublishing.com.

Embrace is an imprint of Entangled Publishing, LLC.

Edited by Lydia Sharp
Cover design by Louisa Maggio
Cover art from iStock

Manufactured in the United States of America

First Edition February 2016

embrace

For a boy I used to know

Whether a thought is spoken or not, it is a real thing and has powers of reality.
The O.C. Bible (p.506, Appendix II)
Dune, Frank Herbert

Raleigh

I promised my brother I'd scatter his ashes on Mars. Not that I believed he'd die before he was old enough to order a beer. I never thought keeping my promise would become impossible, either. Now the urn sits on the mantelpiece, taunting, waiting for me to get my ass off-world. If only it were that easy.

It's hotter than the asshole of hell today, and I'm in a mood to match when the Mulhoney twins saunter into the store. Most people use the self-serve stations, leaving me free to spend my shifts scrolling through the feeds for updates on the MarsLife colony. Not the Mulhoneys.

Vince and Lilah start eying the merchandise, and a sour taste fills my mouth. They've had more brushes with the law than they've got teeth between them, and we have a long tradition of hating each other. Some of Vince's missing teeth are my fault. Though that's hardly the worst of what I've done.

"Hey look, it's the squaw." Lilah nudges her brother and he gives me the finger, sliding it in and out of his mouth. My hands clench into fists, remembering what it felt like smashing his ugly mug. Too bad it didn't erase all the years I'd spent cowering from him and his sister. If anything, I only made it worse.

I try to ignore them and focus instead on the forum posts filling up my NetGlasses. The Earth-huggers are at it again, railing against the evils of Martian pioneers. Mars is the new American dream. There was a time when Europeans looked over the Atlantic and imagined greener pastures. Now, in 2037, all Eartheans gaze into space and imagine interplanetary salvation from our dystopian reality. Us aspiring Martians, we're new order pioneers; dreamers reaching for the stars.

"Got any cheese dicks?" Lilah asks with a straight face while I switch to a thread about the stochastic effects of radiation in the NuRoanoke colony. I bookmark the stream and glare at her over the rim of the glasses. My pulse kicks up a gear and anger simmers in my blood. *Inhale.* Don't lose it. *Exhale.* I've been doing just fine without the meds. *Inhale.* Don't lose it. *Exhale.*

Vince waltzes up to the counter and picks up a pair of the earrings I carved last week.

"Do I look pretty, Roadkill Raleigh?" He holds them to his flappy lobes. "Does it make you wanna bone me?"

"It makes me wanna smash your skull in, plant you in my garden, and let the maggots pick off your flesh so I can use your pelvis as a doorstop."

For a moment there's silence as Vince stares unblinking at me. I didn't mean to say it out loud. My stomach contracts and expands like I'm going to puke.

"Did you just threaten my brother?" Lilah turns scarlet. She reaches over the counter and grabs my hair, slamming my face into the glass. My NetGlasses snap and the two halves skitter to the floor as pain spiderwebs across my cheek. The bell chimes above the door again.

"Remember what happened last time?" Her whispers are acid. "You looking for more of that?"

"What's happening here?" The man's voice booms in a heavy drawl, and it's one I recognize. Now I really want to puke.

"Move along stranger, ain't nothing to see here." Lilah sneers.

"I think it's you who oughta move along." He taps the holster on his hip.

"You a ranger?" Vince smirks.

"Don't need to be to shoot you."

"We're not done, squaw." Lilah dribbles saliva down my cheek. "We got you once; we can get you again." She lets me go with a twist of her fist. The twins stomp out of the store, slamming the door behind them, then tumble into their pickup and roar out of the station. My face aches like I'm going to wake up with a real shiner tomorrow.

"Now that's a lovely young lady." The man offers me a pocket-crushed Kleenex, but I wipe away the spit with my shirt. I don't know his name, and that's the way I'd like to keep it.

"How long you staying in Dead Rock this time?" I ask. There's a tremor in my voice, the rumble before an earthquake. There's still a good chance I'm going to break something.

"A night or two." He grins and rubs the loose ends of my hair between his fingers.

"You looking for something particular?"

"Just the usual, son." His whiskered cheeks pull up in a rictus that sends a chill tip-toeing down my spine.

"Yeah?" For a moment I contemplate refusing, but I need the cash.

"I'll be in all night." He studies me through gray eyes

rimmed in whiskey-red.

"Later then."

"Room 206," he says and dips his Stetson at me before ambling out, heading across the lot to the motel.

Picking up the remains of my NetGlasses, I take a few deep breaths and swallow down my rage. *Don't lose it. Think about what it could cost you…*

MarsLife. I'd give anything for a silver astronaut's pin and a seat on the Entropy III. All I've ever wanted is to stand in that red dust staring out into the unknown, to be part of something bigger, and to be as far away as possible from Dead Rock, Texas. The Corps is holding open aptitude assessments next month. No prior knowledge required. If I pass the tests, I get to attend basic training. But escaping my deadbeat existence doesn't come cheap and earning minimum wage at the Rusty Inn won't be near enough to cover tuition even if I work 24/7. What I got to do to get out of this place sucks, but staying would be worse. Besides, I made a promise to my brother and I intend to keep it.

Mama always said Dead Rock is a cursed place, tainted by all the Indian blood staining the earth. I don't know about Mama's stories, but Dead Rock sure feels cursed all right, a pinprick town everyone's trying to escape. Mama has her craziness, Dad has the Marines, Madison has her son, Weston had his music. And me? Ashes and a dream are all I've got. I only hope it's enough to get me to Mars.

On a Friday night when half the kids I went to high school with have escaped to Amarillo, I'm traipsing up to 206 with a pocket full of condoms. Achieving a dream should be hard, right? If it's too easy, it doesn't seem nearly as worthwhile. This is a means to an end, a way of achieving my dream, the hard part that'll make it all the more worth it. I need money and selling my bone jewelry isn't going to be enough with Dale taking a cut of the profits. This, though, this is *my* money, mine to do with as I please.

I raise my hand to knock on the door as a stream of self-loathing soaks into my soul. This was a whole lot easier when I was dosed up and numb. Without the meds, I feel everything with no way to shut it out. The man answers, his shirt unbuttoned and hanging loose over jeans.

"Knew I'd be seein' you, son." He smirks and gestures for me to come in after he checks left and right that no one's witnessing his indiscretion. "Remind me, how old are you?" he asks, and gulps down another mouthful of whiskey from the tumbler on the nightstand.

"For seven-fifty, I'll be as old as you want me to be." Not knowing my age didn't bother him last time, or the time before that.

He chuckles and sorts through dirty bills. "What'll ten-fifty get me?"

Ten-fifty? That's enough for a new pair of NetGlasses and then some. "Anything you want," I say. "But on one condition."

"Yeah, what's that?" He hands over the cash.

"No talking." I push my earphones in and turn up the volume to max. The angry thrash of guitars drowns out reality as the man unbuttons his fly.

An hour later, I leave the guy passed out across the bed. I button up my jeans and slip out of the room. My body aches all over as if it got pounded by a freight train. Despite the dollars in my pocket, I feel empty, like a black hole that's forgotten it was once a star. Bet my shrink could fix that with drugs faster than a cat could lick its ass.

Whistling for my dog, I head out into the scrub. Bear joins me with a wagging tail and lolling tongue. Together we race through the dust, wind whipping away the stench of sex and the man's cheap aftershave. We pause to catch our breath beneath a blanket of stars that burn much brighter without the moon's glare tonight.

"See that." I point out the constellations to Bear even though he's seen them all before. "That teapot's actually part of Sagittarius and that—" Crouching beside him, I lift his snout so he can look along my finger. "That's Mars. They've got about three hundred people up there building a whole new world. You'd love pouncing around Mars, wouldn't you fella?" He whuffs softly in agreement as I sling my arm around his neck.

The wind drops and in its wake there's a silence thicker than a slice of sheet cake. Even the bugs are holding their breath. A prickle of unease spreads phantom threads along my veins. Bear growls, his hackles up.

"What is it, boy?" I whisper and scan the night, seeing only scattered stars and what might be an airplane heading into Oldham. Bear's growls turn into sorry yelps, tail tucked between his legs, as the light of the plane blossoms into a fractal smear of burning blue.

A meteor? Electricity rips through the air, the hairs on my arms and neck standing stiff with static. There's a tang, too, sweeter than the petro-chemical taint wafting down from the refineries. This smells like ozone and dry ice, like burning metal and fresh blown glass. Seconds later, God flicks on the floodlights and night becomes high noon. A sonic boom follows, and I tumble to my knees, rendered blind and deaf as the pressure wave ripples across the scrub and tears through my mind.

I'm floating, borne on cresting waves of technicolor, wrapped in a nebula of neon. My thoughts scatter, my whole being atomized and cast in a myriad of directions like that time I snapped Madison's friendship bracelet and sent the beads skittering across the kitchen tiles. Only this time it's not beads, but numbers. Ones and zeroes bouncing through the firmament.

Memories race past me in a blur of snapshots. Some I recognize; most disintegrate as soon as I reach for them. Time expands, thick as taffy, pulling me apart, further away from myself until I can't stretch anymore and a scream rips from my throat as I snap back toward the center. An explosion, brighter than any Fourth of July fireworks, fills my vision and knocks me to the ground.

I wake up who knows how long later with Bear licking my face. Dizziness coils around my head and a rash of tingles coats my skin. What the hell just happened? I'm lying in the middle of a crater radiating outward in concentric ridges. I expect a rock, a piece of space junk or some *chido* intergalactic artifact to have fallen from the sky, but lying right beside me is the beat up body of a guy. He wasn't there before the light show. I would've noticed someone sprawled butt naked in the scrub.

For several long moments I stare at the bloodied figure, the wind blasting sand over both of us. Bear moves first, sniffing and licking at the naked corpse. Still feeling frayed around the edges, I haul my ass out of the dirt. My heart's pounding hard enough to crack my ribs as I inch over to the body smeared charcoal and rust.

"Easy now." I nudge Bear as he bashes his nose into the guy's shoulder. A thick crust of blood gloms the side of his face from jaw to eyebrow. I brush away his hair to get a better look. I press two fingers against his neck in search of a pulse, and he groans. Thank God he's still alive.

Gently, I roll him over and starlight spills across his face. He's around my age, a single gash on his head leaking red. Bear licks the wound, and the guy's eyes struggle open. He tries to talk, but his words are garbled. Bruises tie-dye his body beneath a layer of blood and dirt. Where the hell did he come from? It's not like he could've fallen out the sky.

The guy twitches, convulsions quaking up from his feet until his whole body twists and turns.

"I've got you." Tentatively, I hold his shoulders and try to stop his flailing. Struggling to restrain the guy, I wrench my phone from my pocket and call Madison.

"You know what time it is?" she murmurs, her voice thick with sleep.

"Maddy, I need your help."

"Oh God, what happened?" She's wide awake now, the rustle of bed sheets and clothing audible over the phone.

"Head north to McCauley's and bring a blanket." I hang up before she asks for more details.

By the time the pickup's headlights flare across the scrub, the guy is still unconscious. The truck rolls to a stop and Madison leaps out, ruddy ponytail swishing across her shoulders, with a blanket in hand.

"Oh my God, Leigh. What did you do?" She crouches beside me. In the light, the guy's face looks worse, his cheek bruised with grazes along his jaw, and his hair has a purple sheen to it. Madison throws the blanket over the rest of him.

"I didn't do nothing."

"Who is he?" Madison searches my face before pressing two fingers to the guy's wrist. "Did you do this?"

"No!" Not even my own flesh and blood trusts me. "And I don't know who he is. We should get him to the hospital. He had some kind of fit." *Please don't die,* I will the stranger.

"And how you gonna explain this to a doctor when they ask what happened and you're covered in blood?" Madison peels back the guy's eyelids and tilts his head into the light.

"I didn't do it. There was the meteor and then I just found him."

"What meteor?" She scowls.

"How'd you miss it? There was this huge explosion and blinding light."

"You're off your meds, right?"

"I'm not having an episode. I didn't imagine this." Anger fizzes in my veins. Even Madison thinks I'm nuts.

"So you're saying this guy dropped from the sky?" She cocks her head.

"I'm saying I didn't bust his face."

"Like they'll believe it. Let's get him in the truck." She takes his feet and I lift him by the armpits, hefting the majority of his weight as we wrestle his limp body into the pickup.

"Madison." I catch her arm once the guy is propped up in the passenger seat with a second blanket cushioning his head. "I didn't do this."

"Are you sure?" Her over-plucked eyebrows gather above her nose as she gestures to my Lilah-damaged cheek.

"Look." I hold up the back of my hands. No skin missing off my knuckles, but there's blood on my shirt and that'll be more than enough for Sheriff Daniels to toss me behind bars again.

"What happened to your face?"

"Nothing." No point worrying her about the Mulhoney twins.

"Like always, huh?" She shakes her head. "We can't risk it, Leigh. Not while this guy's still out. When he comes round and can tell his version of the story, then we'll see." She swings up into the driver's seat. *We'll see.* So she doesn't quite believe I'm innocent. Guess I deserve her doubt after everything I've done. I hop into the back with Bear, and Madison churns up half the desert doing a U-turn before accelerating toward the Rusty Inn.

She parks outside the motel. Bear and I hop out before she's switched off the engine.

"Why here?" Our family house is only a few hundred yards up the drive, tucked behind the diner.

"You wanna explain to Dale why there's a beat-up, naked stranger on the couch in the morning?" Madison jerks open the passenger door. "We'll use a motel room. You're paying for it."

I'm about to argue, but the look on my sister's face shuts me right up. Together we lug the body into 204 and place him as gently as possible on the bed.

"Get me the first aid kit," Madison says while she prepares for medical ministrations. She got half way through nursing school before she got knocked up, and she's been cleaning me up after fights for years. Stupid kids thought a boy with long hair would be an easy target, but my fists kept proving them wrong.

Leaving Bear outside, I return from the truck with the kit, casting a glance up at the house swamped in shadows. Dale must be asleep, which suits me fine. I'm sick of having to explain myself to Madison's husband. There's a ripple across the darkness that brings on another bout of nausea. Ignoring the dizziness, I hurry back to the room.

Squeeze the antibiotic gel. Hold the gauze. Open the tape. Madison instructs and I obey. After twenty minutes, the guy's face isn't covered in blood anymore. It's dusted with freckles and splotchy bruises. Not even bruises can hide the fact that the guy's gorgeous, with the type of fine features people pay surgeons to sculpt for their faces.

"Stay with him." Madison pulls off medical gloves and shoves them, along with bloody swabs, into the wastepaper basket.

"You mean watch him."

"Leigh, I can't do this." She bites her lip, the creases around her eyes making her look ten years older than she is. "This is your problem now." A frown scrunches up the features she inherited from our father's Welsh ancestors. No one believes she's a quarter Comanche. "Don't forget to pay or Dale'll be down here in the morning."

"What if this guy has another seizure?" Or dies? I did my time in juvie. No way I'm letting them lock me up in federal prison. Things have been getting better. Why'd this guy have to crash land right on top of me?

"Call me," she says. "You know I'll always come when you call." Her smile is sadder than a gopher with half a tail.

"Thanks, Maddy." I activate the app on my phone and transfer a hard-earned hundred bucks to the Rusty Inn for room 204. The panel on the door blinks from "vacant" to "occupied."

She gives my shoulder a quick squeeze before stepping out to the truck. The engine gargles, spluttering biodiesel fumes as she drives it up to its normal spot under the mesquite.

Bear pads into the room, taking up watch by the window before I shut the door. The stranger groans and shifts in his sleep. I settle on the ratty armchair, content to watch from a distance as I search the Web for reports of the meteor. Nada. If a meteor did plummet over Texas, I must be the only soul who saw it. That, or it wasn't a meteor at all.

I press my gloved hand against the glass as if I could trail my fingers through the constellations. The universe is a green screen, just a training simulation, and still my pulse quickens at the thought of what I'm training for.

"The real thing will be beautiful." The words come out of my mouth, but the accent is all wrong.

"Did you do your checks?" my CO asks.

"Three times." I run a hand through my hair, surprised to find springy curls.

I'm dreaming, I'm dreaming, I'm dreaming.

"Initializing cryo-sim." He gestures for me to zip up my overalls then helps me into my cryo-unit. Some people can't handle getting into the pods, claustrophobia and all that. I don't mind the confined space. It feels like being back in the womb.

"How long this time?" I ask.

"Fifty minutes. Ready?"

"Yes."

Am I?

"Sweet dreams." He activates insulation mode, and the glass slides shut, sealing me in a plastic cocoon as chemical mist wraps milky tendrils around my body. One day this will be real, and I'll be going to Mars. The certainty settles over me, and cryo gas floods my lungs, sending me into stasis.

Mars calls to me: a whisper and a promise.

It feels like I've only been asleep for minutes, but morning light spilling through the curtains tells me otherwise. I can still smell the inside of the ship, my stomach in knots at the thought of being en route to the red planet. Just a dream, visceral, vivid, but it wasn't real. I'm not sure it was even me. I've never had a dream like that. The shrink warned me there'd be a period of adjustment coming off the meds. This must be one of the side effects.

Bear whines and thumps his tail. I let him out before checking on the body in the bed. *He* wasn't a dream; Meteor Man exists, his hair splayed across the pillow. He's balled on his side, the covers smeared with dirt. His chest rises and falls with even breathing, and I exhale a sigh of relief. Should I wake him? Leave a note?

A thousand questions swarm inside my skull. Did he really fall out of the sky? Where the hell did he come from?

Who is he? Part of me wants to shake him until the answers spew from his mouth, but the stink of 206 clings to my skin and my shift starts in thirty minutes.

I slip out of the room and head over to the vending machine, spending more hard-earned dollars on this guy. The machine spits out generic overalls and a can of SprayThreads. Not great, but it'll beat having to walk around naked.

He hasn't moved when I creep back into the room. I peer down at him, but his eyes stay shut beneath strands of indigo. His hair looks thick and soft, the kind of hair I want to run my fingers through. My fingers twitch, desperately wanting to sweep the stray curls from his face, but I resist the urge to touch him.

With blood pounding in my ears, I leave the clothes on the side table and ease out of the room. What the hell am I doing? Normalcy is what I need. Routine, the anchor to reality where pretty guys don't take a swan dive into the dirt. And that dream… It's making me feel hungover, my head all fuzzy and my thoughts tangled up like tumbleweed.

I slink up to the house through morning shadows and crawl through my bedroom window. The light in my aquarium paints the posters of Mars on my walls an eerie green. Having fed my fish, I peek into the main bedroom. Madison sprawls across both sides of the bed. Her husband Dale must be down at the diner already prepping his kitchen. You'd think he was a Michelin-starred chef, the pride he takes in serving up Tex-Mex. Quietly, I head into the bathroom, shedding my clothes as I go.

As I step into the shower, my arms prickle, the scars on my wrists smarting like they've just been slashed. They usually only tingle when I walk along the interstate, like maybe Weston's ghost is out there and reaching for my hand. But today, on the anniversary of his death, they don't just tingle, they burn. I used to open up the seams every year on this day, but my bleeding never changed anything, and it only upset Madison who ended up having to disinfect and bandage them.

The water scalds my skin and steam fills up the bathroom. Gritting my teeth against the sting, I turn up the heat some more, but it isn't hot enough to wash away the memory of 206. Angry tracks cut across my back from his nails. There are bite marks on my shoulders and carpet burns on my knees. Ten-fifty. Is that all I'm worth?

The steam in the shower looks a lot like the cryo-mist in the stasis pod. I can still taste it—minty with a chemical tang. Sure, I've read enough about Mars to dream the whole process in detail, but that was different, crisp and logical, not like the confusion of dreams. It was more like a memory... That's impossible.

Having tugged on clean clothes, I check on my nephew. Nash lies curled up in his cot with his thumb in his mouth, safe, sleepy, and loved. Did I ever look like that? Quietly, I duck out of the house and head down to the diner, kicking an old football through the dirt for Bear. I haven't been outside five minutes and I'm already sweating. The sun's shining like it couldn't give a shit about my brother's anniversary, like a clear blue sky makes everything okay.

Halfway down the path, there's a crow's feather snagged in a knot of creosote. I braid my sweat-sticky hair and tie the feather into the end. West had a crow's feather tattoo on his chest, one where the tip of the feather burst into more tiny birds. He said it was a symbol of freedom. I guess death is a kind of freedom.

"Late." Dale points an accusatory finger at me, his bloodshot eyes bulging out of his head when I stomp into the kitchen. "And what in God's green country is that?" He yanks at the feather. "You must be slower than molasses on a cold day bringin' that shit in here."

"It's for West."

For a moment his expression softens and he lets go of my hair, grown long again since I hacked it short for West's funeral, then it's back to business. Dale returns to his grill, mumbling about hygiene standards, but he makes no comment about Madison's late-night excursion. While prepping my automatons, I scroll through newsfeeds on my phone. Zip, zero, nada about meteors. Not even a hokey claim about a UFO sighting. But I didn't imagine it. How could I have been the only one to see him fall? I post a question about it on the MarsLife message board—that's bound to get a few hits—and resign myself to waiting.

"Mornin'." Abigail breezes into the kitchen with empty salt shakers. "So, Raw." She pins me with a stare that says she hasn't forgotten what day it is. "Got anything new for me today?" She flips blonde hair over her shoulder and gives me a sad smile as she hands the shakers over to Bob the pantry-bot. It manages to spill almost as much as it fills with its outdated phalanges, but we can't afford a newer model.

"Mars has the tallest mountain in the solar system," I start. "Olympus Mons, a shield volcano." A grin tugs at my lips imagining what it must look like rising out of the red as I sweep up spilled salt.

"How tall?" Abi asks, still willing to talk to me even when she knows almost everything about me. She knows not to mention West. Neither of us wants to talk about him today. We can't, not when we still hurt so much.

"Don't encourage him," Dale barks from the grill where he's flipping burgers despite Tim, the grill-bot, standing at the ready with an egg lifter.

"Twenty-seven kilometers." I glare at Dale. "Which is almost seventeen miles. Straight up in the air."

"Yeah and knowing that's about as useful as a strawberry up a bear's butt. You think they're gonna take a crazy kid with a record up to Mars?" Dale's words hit me like a baseball bat to the balls. Knowing everything about Mars doesn't help a penny if I don't make it past the first round of admission tests. There's nothing I can do about the record except prove that I've changed, changed enough to stand in the stasis habitat onboard an interplanetary ship coasting through white and gold stars.

"Why don't you join Abi at AC and make something of your life?" Dale says with nothing but good intentions. We've had this conversation before, about me going to school, but Dale doesn't get it. He never has.

"I am making something of my life."

"By going to Mars? Wake up, son." He brandishes the burger tongs.

"Ignore him," Abi says. "He's just sore because he don't know half of what you do and they don't teach none of that at AC." She gathers the salt shakers and departs with a wink and a swish of her fractal-patterned skirt. Dale says something about how it's time I start acting like the grown man that I am and stop living off my sister, but I ignore him.

Earphones couched in my ears, I slip away from reality. A temporary escape: stories about other times and other planets, words that take me far away from the drudgery of my life. I'm on Arrakis, riding sand-worms with Muad'Dib while monitoring the efficacy of Suds the dishwashing-bot. There's got to be more to life than making sure robots don't screw up menial tasks, but I won't find it on Earth.

METEOR MAN

```
tech1@cer-ro:~$   chmod   +x   psytek-2.14.8   &&   ./
psytek-2.14.8 p=torres@cer-ro:/lab1/RW
```

The worst sound in the world is the dying squeal of a dog. I'm eight years old again, and my father's hands are on my shoulders, forcing me to watch two pit bulls tear each other apart.

Ugly black hatred boils in my heart. Hatred for what my father is making me watch, hatred for the kids at school who send me home with bruises, hatred for myself and the tears welling in my eyes.

My brother slips his hand into mine when Dad is too caught up in the final moments of the fight to pay us any attention. I want to look away, but I can't even blink as the smaller dog gets mauled.

"Quit your bawling." Dad smacks me across the back of the head. This whole trip is meant to toughen me up, to stop me being such a pussy and letting the other kids pick on me at school. My brother loops his arm around my shoulders when they drag the dead dog away. They rinse down the arena for the next round, and my fried-chicken dinner threatens to make a reappearance.

I'm awake. My naked body trembles. Two hands, two feet. I wiggle my toes.

The time is 11:43 a.m.

I do not know where I am.

I survey my surroundings. Bed. Table. Chair. Wall-screen.

Motel room, then.

Lying still, my senses provide stimuli to my brain, and I parse the information, becoming more aware.

The smell of dog's blood sticks in my nose. A dream. A memory.

Slowly, I ease myself into a sitting position. Fire in my ribs and down my back. Pain blinds me. Then fades.

```
tech1@cer-ro:~$ sudo apt-get update
```

The headache pulses, intensifying every time I move. Every few seconds it feels like…like Hiroshima inside my skull.

I'm wearing nothing but my own blood. I'm filthy.

Clothes, I need clothes.

There's a pair of plastic wrapped overalls and canned cotton on the side table.

I need a shower.

Wincing with every footfall, I take tentative steps toward the bathroom. The image of a newborn giraffe flashes through my mind.

I stink, a mix of burning metal and roadkill.

I scrub at my skin and hair with the soap dispensed from a plastic wall unit. Warm water down my back. It feels good. I close my eyes and tilt my face into the spray.

Who am I?

```
tech1@cer-ro:~$ sudo apt-get upgrade
```

The blood and dust wash away, a rust-brown spiral disappearing down the drain.

There are marks on my body. Someone's carved me up like a Jack 'o Lantern. The symbols on my chest look like something out of a grimoire. The scars aren't random either, forming symmetrical lines down each side of my body.

I'm lean and wiry. A bigger man could've got the jump on me and cut me up. Or maybe they drugged me and that's why it feels like World War III between my ears. Maybe *I'm* the one who likes getting cut up and got these marks done to myself.

The face in the mirror is a stranger's.

Purple hair and green eyes. Freckles across my nose and shoulders. I'm no stranger to the sun.

The sweltering, blister-gaze of the sun... The headache goes supernova.

I'm on the football field running drills. Sweat runs rivers down our faces, but Coach doesn't let up, making us sprint and tackle even as the mercury soars into the hundreds. My face is on fire and every breath is like French kissing a tailpipe. I hate every minute of practice, hate every brutal moment, but maybe Dad'll finally be proud. That's why I play...


```
tech1@cer-ro:~$ reboot
```


I retch into the toilet, puking out what little is in my gut. The headache retreats and my vision clears as I rinse my mouth. So my dad took me to see dog fights to toughen me up, and I played football to impress him. Charming childhood. No wonder I'm in this motel minus a fully functioning memory.

Drugs, man, it must've been drugs. But…pit bulls and football… Somehow the memory fits more like a borrowed shirt.

There's bruising at my temple and grazes on my jaw. Brain trauma. That explains why I'm incoherent and why I can't remember. The screen on the wall offers me a vast selection of entertainment, but says nothing about who I am.

Time to slip this joint and find some answers.

I flap my arms getting the spray-on shirt to dry faster before hauling on the overalls. What about shoes? I finish the can of SprayThreads, embalming my feet and giving the soles a few extra layers.

Taking a deep breath, I crack open the door.

The heat is a suffocating deluge. A diner called the Rusty Inn sits across the parking lot to the right. To the left, a gas station and store with a wonky sign reading RECEPTION dangling from a single nail above. Beyond that lies the road, snaking through the mirage-hazed scrub toward the highway. The roar of trucks and traffic provides a constant accompaniment.

Where the hell am I?

I could be in the middle of the Australian Outback for all I know. I take cautious steps across the baking tar toward the pumps. I head to the store, which doubles as motel reception, in the hopes of finding a human being to talk to. The shop is deserted except for a woman behind the counter. She pales at my approach, her fingers shredding a gum wrapper.

"Morning." I test my voice. It cracks and husks.

"You," she says, clearly nervous. "What do you want?" She sounds afraid. Of me? A sour unpleasantness churns in my belly. Her name tag reads Madison.

"Um…" I lower my voice and take a few steps closer. "I just want to know what happened to me."

She backs away and her hand reaches under the counter. For a rifle, a panic button? I'm not keen on either of those.

"Please, Madison." I raise my open hands. "I just want to know—"

"I don't know and I can't do any more for you. You should leave." Her expression hardens. "You got no business being here."

"Can't you at least tell me—" My name, where I am... anything? But she doesn't let me finish.

"What'll it take to get you to leave?" She opens the cash register and riffles through dirty old bills. "Here. Please, just leave us out of this." There's hardly more than a hundred dollars there, and she's scooping it all up.

"I don't want your money." Christ, I feel like a criminal now. Maybe I am. "I'm sorry. Truly, this was all just a misunderstanding." I flee from the store and almost get hit by a station wagon with Arizona plates as it pulls up for gas. Arizona—that explains the heat and maybe it explains my freckles. There's an elderly couple in the car. The man gets out to fill his tank.

"You all right, son?" He gestures to my contused temple.

"Actually, I was wondering if you could give me a lift." I cast a nervous glance over my shoulder at the woman at the counter, still watching me, her face pinched with concern.

"Where to?" His jaw works on gum or tobacco.

Hospital? Police station? Clearly I was robbed and someone beat me senseless so I should be reporting it, and maybe there's a missing persons report that'll tell me my name. Or maybe it was a drug deal gone wrong and the carvings on my skin are gang symbols. I could be handing myself over to the pigs. Don't know much, but I know I don't want to be behind bars. And Madison must have a pretty good reason to want me gone, if only she'd tell me.

"Which way you headed?" I ask, not that it matters.

"Up to Oklahoma. We can drop you at the Mercy General in Amarillo if you want. You don't look too good."

"Amarillo?"

"Closest ER 'round these parts."

"These parts?" Where am I?

"Dead Rock, Texas, son. Are you sure you're all right?"

I squint at the sky. A huge blue blanket frayed at the edges with cloud. Texas.

"If you don't mind taking me to Amarillo, sir, I'd really appreciate it."

He nods and I clamber into the back, making nice with his obese wife, grateful for the AC if not for the prehistoric country music lambasting my ears. Pit bulls, football, and a distaste for country music—now all I need is a name.

The farther we drive from Dead Rock, the worse the headache becomes, skewering me at the temple and filling my vision with a dozen pulsing stars. I press the heels of my hands against my eyes, and they come away wet. With blood. Jesus Christ, I'm bleeding from my eyes!

"Drive faster, Tony." The wife batters her husband's arm, and he steps on the gas. She hands me a paper towel, but it doesn't do much to stem the tide pouring from my eyes and now my nose.

Hemorrhage. I could be a freaking hemophiliac for all I know. These could be my last moments before I bleed out on the backseat of Tony and Mary-Jo's station wagon. What a way to go, complete with a soundtrack courtesy of geriatric Tim McGraw.

Time expands and contracts. I'm floating and the pain in my head blossoms into an agony I have no words for.

I'm six years old and it's Wednesday afternoon in the middle of a September that thinks it's July. My brother strides into our bedroom, his T-shirt stained with sweat and peanut butter.

"Look what I found." He sits beside me on the floor, shoving LEGO bricks out of the way. My baby-fat fingers grip the plastic blocks, my knees scabbed from tumbling off my bike. My hair is cut short, shaved at the back like my brother's.

"Hey, you listening, buddy?" He nudges me with an elbow and smiles, his teeth jutting out at all angles.

"Yeah?"

"Look. New images from the Endeavor." He taps the screen of his SchoolPro900, zooming in on the image of Mars. "They sent this rover out from the colony," he says. "Impressive, huh?"

I press my fingers to the screen, imagining that hot red sand burning my skin.

"Whoa." My little mind — perhaps not my mind at all — struggles to grasp how I'm seeing pictures of another planet on my brother's palmtop computer while sitting on the floor in Dead Rock, Texas.

"Yup. There's video, too." My brother — Weston — opens a new tab and hits play. The first of the MarsLife colonizers, bouncing around in the regolith, kicking a soccer ball back and forth. They're smiling, they're happy, and the Martian sunset turns the brown sky as blue as Texas bluebonnets.

"I wanna go to Mars."

"Better start savin' up now. Tourist tickets are like a bazillion dollars." Weston gives me the serious face he wears when I ask to play with his model airplanes.

"I want to be an astronaut." I point at the screen, at the men and women jump-floating around the reflective huts crouched like beetles on the surface of the planet.

"Sure you do." He musses my hair. "You ever gonna be smart enough, like me?"

"'Course." I push him away. He tackles me and we're wrestling on the floor, rolling over LEGO bricks and shrieking with pain. Our game comes to an end at the sound of cracking glass. Turns out SchoolPros aren't as durable as they claim. A six-year-old's weight and a handful of plastic blocks is enough to break the screen. The astronauts are still laughing despite the spiderweb fracture across the LCD.

We both stare at the damage, knowing one of us will have to take the blame, knowing one of us will have to pay when our father finds out. Not that it really matters. It's always Weston's fault, never mine.

"I'm sorry, West." There are tears in my voice.

"It was an accident," he says. "Dad can't be mad about an accident." Except we both know he can and he will. One of us will get the belt and, except for that one time when I threw the baseball through the window right in front of Dad, it's always West.

"Better 'fess up and get it over with." Weston sighs and gets to his feet.

The fear is a live animal, a sharp twisting in my belly when I think what Dad will do to Weston, how it should be me getting the belt and how grateful I am it won't be. Guilt and anger and regret tornado inside of me, filling me up until I feel like I'm going to explode.

I'm going to explode!

"Pull over!" I cup my hands over my mouth and scrabble at the handle. Throwing open the door, I start spewing before the car comes to a stop. Blood and bile splatter the dust.

"We should call an ambulance, Tony. Call them." Mary-Jo fusses over me, her plump fingers on the back of my neck. I stagger out of the car, away from her clammy hands. Hooray for a new memory. My dad was a bastard and I was a coward. I think I liked myself better when I didn't know who I was.

Dead Rock, Texas.

Despite my accent not being what I'd expect, I guess Dead Rock is home. Or used to be. At any rate, it's the only clue I've got.

"I have to go back." With my arms wrapped around my churning middle, I stare at Tony and he fumbles with his phone. "Take me back."

"You need to go to the hospital." Mary-Jo waddles toward me, waving Kleenex at me.

"You don't understand. I need to go back."

"Listen, son. You need a doctor, and we'll take you to one, but we're not going back." Tony gets stern.

"No worries. Thanks anyway." I turn my back on them and stagger along the shoulder, watching where I put my feet. Behind me, Mary-Jo and Tony argue philanthropy versus common sense, but common sense prevails and they drive away. In my sorry state no one's going to give me a ride back to deadbeat Dead Rock. Maybe I was infected with Ebola or something equally nasty and left to die. My imagination runs wild, conjuring a hundred thousand scenarios. None of them stick. None of them make any sense.

It's a long walk back to town. If someone sees me all bloody faced, they're bound to call the cops, if Tony and Mary-Jo haven't already. I ditch the highway in favor of the service road beside it and head west. I'm probably imagining it, but with every step I take toward Dead Rock, the pain in my head seems to ease. Maybe I am going home.

Raleigh

Grabbing an extra burger and fries, I head up to 204. I knock, but there's no answer. Maybe he took off, and I'll never see him again. Or maybe he's dead. *God, please don't let him be dead.* That's the last thing any of us needs. I let myself in.

The drapes are drawn and the bed is empty. The clothes are gone, too. I check the bathroom to make sure he hasn't passed out in the shower. He's gone. But I didn't imagine it. The sheets are stained brown and burgundy, and Maddy's blanket lies crumpled on the floor. He was real; he was here. I strip the bed and bundle up the used towel, lugging everything to the adjacent maintenance building and hand it all to Rosie the laundry-bot. She obliges with a hiss of aging knee joints and I return to the kitchen, tossing Bear the extra burger meal.

It's after seven by the time I finish my shift. Grabbing a bottle of bourbon from the bar when Dale's not looking, Bear and I jog to the interstate.

Meteor Man. A thousand questions smolder on the back of my tongue, but I swallow them. No good wishing the guy was around to answer them when he isn't. Besides, it's time to visit my brother.

The Texas sky stretches an empty hand across the desert, reaching for the shimmer-slick horizon it won't ever be able to hold. Bear and I hit the dirt road cutting between the fracking lands flanking old McCauley's farm. It's not even a farm anymore, just a homestead crumbling down around a geriatric couple too stubborn to sell their land before they kick the bucket.

My feet lead me straight to the crater. Pain drills

through the side of my skull, a screwdriver to the brain as a kaleidoscope of images form and fracture in my mind: Writing a final physics exam and not knowing all the answers, meeting my little sister's first boyfriend, struggling against the effects of zero gravity.

The mental storm ends when I blink. What's happening to me? Withdrawal from the meds shouldn't be like this, not this intense or disorientating. This is more like a bad acid trip. How can I remember something I've never done? *Please don't let this be another episode.*

Chilled despite the baking heat, I turn away from the crater and head back to the interstate, the headache fading. McCauley's drought-slimmed cattle are ghost smudges in the dusk heat as Bear and I follow the trail of roadkill along the asphalt. The wind barrels across the land, drenching us in the stench of gasoline from the lonely pump-jacks studding the fields to the north. We approach the bone cross marking the spot where Weston met his maker and my scars start to burn.

First time I made the cuts right after West died, everyone thought I was trying to kill myself. I tried telling them it was Comanche tradition, a way of honoring the dead, but all that got me was another prescription for meds I'm not sure I ever needed. They gave me the wrong cocktail, too. Instead of the drugs making me happy, they made me crazy: make Daddy Sergeant Williams proud, throw sick bullets and score touchdowns, beat a kid's head in and get sent to juvie kind of crazy.

I brush bird shit off the bleached leg bones of a coyote with the hem of my shirt and splash bourbon into the dried-out grass. My brother chose suicide over standing up to our father. Hope Dad enjoys hunting down insurgents in the Middle East while his eldest son sits in an urn on the mantelpiece.

"Hi, West," I whisper. "Here's to four years dead."

Four years since he took Dad's shiny Dodge and plowed it into a rig tearing toward Amarillo. They called it an accident, but West was tired of being a disappointment. There was only so much he could take before he left for the Happy Hunting Ground of our ancestors.

A black SUV slows down a little as it passes me, the occupants invisible behind tinted windows. I ignore it and they accelerate, tires spinning through the sludge of roadkill slicking the asphalt. Bear trots past me and tears into the sloppy carcass of a jackrabbit.

"Leave it!" My voice is hoarse, my lips parched. He whines in protest but bounds over to me, his tail wagging and tongue lolling. It's hot enough to give a rattlesnake sunburn out here. I slake my thirst with a swig of bourbon.

"Nothing online about the meteor," I tell West. "The guy is real enough. Maybe they've been right all along and I am crazy." Crazy angry, crazy sad, crazy desperate to get off this planet and make something of my life.

The bourbon is too tempting. I like it far too much. After taking one last swallow, I toss the bottle across the road with my QB arm and a rig blows its horn as it hurtles for New Mexico. I've never even left Texas, never wanted to go anywhere but up. I squint, trying to glimpse the stars, but the dying sun burns up the sky, cutting streaks of red and orange across the tattered clouds.

Bear barks away a bunch of buzzards feasting up ahead and I follow. The armadillo's pretty fresh with only the skull crushed, the shell mostly intact and stinking to high heaven. Bear helps, and together we pry the carcass from the tarmac. It only just fits into my roadkill bag.

"What are you doing?" The voice startles me so hard I drop the armadillo, the shell slamming into my toe. One-footed, I turn to face Meteor Man. He's standing a few feet away near the bridge where the I-40 crosses a dirt service road, hands in the pockets of the overalls, his hair falling across red-rimmed eyes. His feet don't look too good, with bits of bloodied SprayThreads trailing in the dust. He follows my gaze and mutters something about having no shoes. That's my fault, but if he hadn't run off, I could've found him a pair.

"How'd you find me?" If he'd been following me, I would've seen him. He hikes up the embankment near the bridge, joining me on the shoulder. Maybe I should be creeped out by his sudden appearance, but I'm glad to see the guy alive. I'm glad to see him period, even if that makes no sense.

"Do I know you?" His accent is all silk and smooth edges. Nothing like my Texan drawl.

"You don't remember?"

"Should I?" He folds to the ground and inspects his damaged feet. Bear trots up to him and proceeds to give him a face wash. Full lips and green eyes, a cluster of freckles on his left temple that spill over his nose and dimpled chin. He drags a hand through his hair, and I'm jealous of his fingers. My pulse ratchets up a gear when he catches me staring.

"What do you remember?" I lower my gaze and my hands clench into instinctual fists. Aside from the occasional rig, we're alone out here. *Inhale.* He's unarmed and the chances of him getting the drop on me are next to nothing. *Exhale.* All banged up like that he's in no state to fight. *Inhale.* And this time I would fight back. *Exhale.*

"Not much. I woke up in the motel down the road. Do you know it?" He pushes Bear away. Without all the blood on his face, the bruises don't look half bad. He heals fast.

"Yeah." My gaze returns to his freckles, and I swallow hard. "That's my place."

"Yours?" He squints up at me through his purple fringe.

"My sister's. We found you in the desert last night and took you back to the motel."

"You found me?" Doesn't sound like he believes me.

"All beat up. I think you..." I suck in a breath, wondering how crazy he'll think I am for telling him about the meteor.

"What?" He flicks hair off his face and fixes me with an intense stare.

"There was a meteor, and then suddenly there you were, naked on the ground."

"You think I hitched a ride here from outer space?" His smile is lopsided, and I answer it with a shrug.

"My sister patched you up."

"Ah-huh." His smile evaporates. "Does she work at the gas station?"

"Sometimes. Why?"

"Just wondering." His tongue darts between his lips, lapping at a bead of blood oozing from the sun-dried corner of his mouth. For a moment I forget to breathe.

"Listen, I just found you," I manage to say when he raises his eyebrows expectantly. I'm staring again. "I had nothing to do with whatever happened, okay?"

"Okay." He cocks his head, considering.

"You don't believe me?"

"I think I do. Did you leave the clothes for me?"

"Yup. Sorry I forgot about shoes." Why the heck am I apologizing? Seeing this guy bleed is making me feel all kinds of guilty for no good reason.

"Do you know who I am?"

"Not a clue."

"Do you know who did this to me?"

"Like I said, I found you all beat up alone just laying in the dirt." I double check my knuckles to be sure and release my fists. It's been fifteen months since I hit someone.

"What's your name?"

"Raleigh."

"Raw-lee." He tries to mimic my drawl.

"Like the city." A place Mama's never been. Same way

she's never been to Madison County or Weston, Florida either. I hope I never have a kid called Mars. "Do you have a name?" I crouch beside him. There's a spark of energy between us that's far more intense than the hormonal gush of lust at first sight. It's electric and terrifying. Does he feel it, too? He must. The hairs on the back of my neck stand at attention, trepidation bolting down my spine.

"I'm sure I do," he says. "Not that I can remember it."

"I'll have to call you something."

"As long as it's not Buck or Billy-Bob." He tosses me a grin and some of the tension drains out of my shoulders. I relax my grip on the armadillo bag.

The wind teases my hair and the feather I picked up this morning brushes against my cheek. "How about Crow?"

"Bird of death, correct?" His gaze rests on the feather fluttering against my face.

"Among other things." Transitional magic, shape-shifting, and trickery, too. A suitable name any which way.

"I like it. Crow." He smiles and offers me his hand. "Pleased to meet you, Raleigh." We shake and the contact sends an electric shock up my arm, which explodes behind my eyes. *Building sandcastles on a shell-strewn beach, waves crashing violently against the shore, and gulls screaming.* The images assault my mind. He gasps and jerks his hand away. The ocean scene fades.

"You okay?" I ask, my mouth drier than the Mojave. Crow looks like he might puke.

"What the fuck was that?" He swallows hard and blinks away tears, massaging his hand where we touched. I want to know if he saw something, too, but there's no asking that without sounding like a total nutjob, especially if his answer is no. Whoever, *what*ever this guy is, I've got to figure out. I've never seen the ocean, so there's no way that scene came out of my head, yet I could taste the salt in the air and feel the sand between my toes like it was me standing in the surf.

"Static electricity. It's real dry out here." Better to play it safe.

"Right." He flicks hair from his eyes. God, he's gorgeous, even all banged up. I'm staring. I could stare all day, but lingering out here is going to turn us into puddles of melted flesh.

"You never answered my question." He nudges the bag with his toe.

"I make stuff from the bones." No need for him to know it was doing penance for beating up Vince that first got me picking up corpses. That's what happens when you hit a kid with a daddy in law enforcement. Never mind that that kid stole my lunch money for years, gave me more swirlies than I care to remember on his sister's orders, and even cut up my brand new pair of Nikes once. I guess I should've been grateful he tore my shoes off my feet before going to town with his pocket knife.

"Like what?" Crow asks, and I shake off the bad memories of elementary school.

"Jewelry, wind chimes. I don't know. Stuff." I shrug. "I'm heading back to town. Think you can make it?"

"If not, you look like you could carry me." He flashes me another smile, his gaze lingering on my biceps and pecs, and now the heat flooding my veins has nothing to do with the day being 98 degrees.

He's still looking at me, but I say nothing. I don't trust myself to speak. We keep walking, Crow limping and Bear trotting beside me.

"Who died?" Crow asks when we pass the bone cross.

"My brother." The words are a whisper.

"I had a brother, or have, I think." He pauses at the coyote bones. "It's all a bit fuzzy. It comes to me in bits and pieces."

Like when we shook hands? But I don't ask. At least he

hasn't apologized. First reaction to finding out I've got a dead brother is always "I'm sorry," but I've never wanted sympathy. Platitudes never changed a thing.

After a few yards of silence he asks, "How old are you?"

"Nineteen."

"Are you studying?" Crow licks his lips, parched from the heat.

"You know, for a guy who can't remember shit about himself, you sure seem real interested in me." There's no hiding the irritation in my voice. If only the answers could go both ways, I might not mind getting the third degree.

"Sorry." He holds up his hands. "No more questions."

We walk in silence again until Crow clears his throat.

"Look, you found me. You're the only person I know. Will you help me, Raleigh?" He looks at me the same way Bear does when I'm eating bacon; that look makes my bones melt faster than the Texas sun.

I could help him, but at what cost?

"Wow, look at that." His gaze slips past my shoulder to the celestial body rising above the skyline. "That's Mars. Did you know a guy who weighs ninety kilos on Earth would only weigh thirty-three on Mars?"

"You can remember that, but not your zip code?" That he knows about Mars sends heat ratcheting up my spine. *It was just a dream.*

"Apparently." He shrugs and stuffs his hands into his pockets.

"Actually, it's thirty-three point nine kilograms on Mars. To be precise," I say.

"You're right." He grins. "So will you help me?"

My turn to shrug. "Depends what it involves. I don't want any trouble." I'm not the person he needs, and I certainly don't need some memory-less drifter in my life right now. One more month of staying out of trouble and maybe I'll make it through the aptitude tests, record and all.

"Yeah, I understand. How about this: you help me, but if things go awry, I won't blame you for wanting out. Deal?" He offers me his hand and gingerly we shake, his fingers grazing the keloid on my wrist. Crow makes no comment about my scars and no weird images tumble through my mind this time, although his touch does make my fingers tingle.

"You sound like you're from the West Coast. That's a start, right?" I slow my pace to match Crow's hobble.

"I guess."

"You might want to see a doctor." That head injury could've been worse than Madison thought. Guilt gives my insides acupuncture. It was entirely selfish not to get him proper help last night. The guy could've died and then what? Bury him in my roadkill garden?

"Already tried," he says. "It didn't work out so well."

"Is that where you went?"

"Yup, tried to hitch into Amarillo, but halfway there my head went nuclear and my eyes started bleeding."

"Shit." That sounds serious, like he should be getting admitted and not strolling 'round the desert. "Why'd you come back here?"

"I had this memory about my childhood in Dead Rock and it just felt right. As soon as I started walking back, I stopped crying blood and the headache went away."

"You think you grew up here?" I'd know him if he had.

"Who knows, but I do know I need to be here. The answers are in Dead Rock. Besides, who'd believe I fell from the sky?" A wry smile tugs at his lips.

"Your choice."

"Thanks, but I think I'm okay, although that only makes this more weird." His feet scuff through the dirt, trailing shreds of SprayThreads. "Why didn't you call the cops when you found me?" That's the question I've been dreading.

What answer would he prefer? Because I'm a juvie kid who has a history of trouble with the law. Because the sheriff's got it in for me ever since I knocked his nephew's teeth out. Because I'm screwing for money and want out of this town and off this planet without the trouble another police report would bring.

"I was kinda freaked out about you crash landing." My words come out shakier than I like. "Thought you might be an alien." No I didn't, but now it doesn't seem that impossible.

"Really?" Crow raises both eyebrows at me.

"You look human enough."

"Probably not from Texas, and maybe human." He chews on his thumb. There's fear in his eyes, a fear I can relate to. "Not a lot to go on."

"Why didn't you go to the cops?" If I'd woken banged up and naked in a strange place, would my first stop have been the cops? Doubtful.

"No, man, not until I know more about what happened. Please, Raleigh. Help me." I find myself nodding despite my gut yelling at me to run—except I can't tell if it's to run away from Crow, or toward him.

CROW

Crow. At least I have a name now. Not that it helps me feel any more like myself. But a name is a good start; it makes me feel more human despite the strange symbols littering my skin and my propensity for sanguine pyrotechnics.

When Raleigh shook my hand, I saw something, a flash of memory or a cracked piece of dream. I was lying on the warm roof of a clapped-out car, lying next to my brother and watching the stars. No, a meteor shower. We were talking about the speed of light and how we're looking at the past and my accent had the slow motion drawl of Raleigh's. The vision stopped as abruptly as our handshake. It must be the head injury. The brain trauma must've short circuited my synapses. That's the only rational explanation.

Standing in the dark outside my motel room staring at the stars, it makes me wonder if any of this is real at all or if it's the product of some weird dissociative coma and my broken brain is dreaming all this up: the hot dust coating borrowed shoes, the wide sky, the ruler straight road bisecting it all and there, hanging like an ax in the sky, is Mars.

"Are these readings normal?" A snatch of conversation carries on the breeze.

"Brain function is nominal but..." the voice fades into static, returning a moment later. **"It's too soon to tell. I'm logging the anomalies and charting their development."**

I scan the lot, but there's no one around. Must be the echoes of an entertainment unit from one of the other rooms.

"I want a report on my desk by tomorrow... Prepare the termination protocols."

"That won't be necessary."

I ignore the voices and focus on the stars. Mars. The red planet has a mass of about 642 billion kilograms. It has two moons, Phobos and Deimos. Mars has the largest dust storms in the solar system, some lasting for several months, and the most severe seasonal changes due to an elongated elliptical orbit. How can I remember all that and not my own name?

Turning my back on Mars, I step into the air-conditioned box and ditch my shirt, letting the cold air raise goose bumps on my skin. I rub at the marks on my body, the scars a purplish-pink. Deliberately and equidistantly spaced from my shoulders down the length of my body, the scars must mean something. Smaller knots dot my arms and legs as well. The highest concentration is on my back, meandering down my spine from a larger knot on the back of my neck.

Accessing the 'net, I run a few image searches looking for occult symbols that might bear a resemblance to the one on my skin. No such luck. Next, I check through religious symbols from Zoroastrianism to neo-paganism. Still nothing. Desperate, I search through alphabets of dead and extant languages. None of the alphabets are a good match for the spiraling motif cut into my flesh. Cuneiform might come closest but doesn't provide any meaningful answers. I slam my fist into the wall as if the shock of pain will somehow jolt my memories back into place. It's no surprise when all I get is a sore hand.

Another hour spent searching and no missing persons match my description, at least not in Texas. If I could only remember my name, I could search for myself and no doubt half a dozen social media sites would pop up holding the answers to who I am. Image search! Clearly my recent head trauma killed a few brain cells.

The motel screen doesn't have a camera. Hah, I can only imagine the type of pornos that might get recorded if it did. I'm halfway out the door and ready to bang on Raleigh's when I glimpse the time. It's after one a.m. One more night of not knowing isn't going to kill me. I hope. My plan can wait until tomorrow.

"Is he a threat to the system?" The voices are back.

"No. This is a rare opportunity, let's…" Static gobbles up the last syllables.

"Monitor this situation closely. We need viable results."

"You think I don't know that?" The second voice snaps before fading altogether as if they're coming down some long-distance telephone line. Numbness spreads from my feet, up my legs, and into my chest. My hands turn transparent, the symbols on my arms a curling knot of—

tech1@cer-ro:~$ reboot

Raleigh

A woman at the podium calls my name. I can't make out the words, but my body reacts of its own volition and I stride to the stage. The crowd applauds. The woman smiles and holds my award, a silver trophy for outstanding academic achievement.

My mom and dad sit off to the side, clapping and smiling. They're proud of me, and my chest swells until it feels like I'm walking on clouds. With a smile, I accept the trophy like it's a Nobel Prize. Maybe one day, it will be. My heart pounds, the blood throbbing in my ears. The pounding grows louder until it feels like there's a fist bashing against my skull.

"You awake?" Dale bangs on my door. "We're going to church," he says louder than necessary. "Get your ass outta that bed and down to the diner."

"Coming." I grumble. There should be a law against getting up at 7 a.m. on a Sunday.

"Make sure that bot don't burn the burgers." Dale's feet stomp down the hallway as I roll out of the covers. Academic trophies?

I shake off the remnants of the dream and tug on a clean T-shirt that Rosie must've forgotten in the dryer. It's shrunk and molds to my body. I hated playing football, but I don't mind what it did to my physique, giving me ripped arms and abs, and a decent amount of strength I've managed to maintain with a regimen of push-ups and sit-ups. I consider changing into something my size, but I liked the way Crow looked at me, like he enjoyed what he was seeing without knowing it only costs others a few hundred dollars to touch. Maybe he'll look at me like that again.

I head out back to the roadkill cemetery sprawled

beneath a pair of mesquites. For once, Bear hasn't dug up the fresh body, leaving my armadillo to rot in peace. It'll take at least a month for the worms to strip the flesh off the bones. The coyote remains I got back in spring are almost ready to be boiled and bleached. They'll make a fine set of chimes.

Bear lopes up, tail wagging and strands of drool dangling from his lips. Crow follows. He's sprayed on a new black T-shirt, and it shows off his biceps as well as pale tattoos. They're like creeper winding from shoulders to wrists, with what I think might be roses dotted between wrist and elbow.

Except, his skin is raised, almost like the patterns have been embossed. My fingers find the marks on my wrists. No doubt about it. Crow isn't sporting ink, but scars.

"You're up early." Giving Bear a pat, I reach for the hose and start soaking the graves.

"Couldn't sleep." Crow squints up at the trees that don't provide much shade. "Why do you water the corpses?" He crouches down and steals sideways glances at me. I'm glad I stuck with this shirt.

"Maybe they'll sprout roots and grow into bone trees. Maybe I'll turn this whole stretch into a skeleton orchard."

"A roadkill garden." He grins, and, as I continue to wet the ground, I'm painfully aware of our arms less than an inch away from touching. He smells good, too. Beneath the layer of cheap motel soap and chemical cotton he smells of something not from Dead Rock, of something the desert hasn't sandblasted and the sun hasn't fried to a crisp.

"Would be kinda neat, right?"

"Or macabre." Crow drags a finger through the mud and hair falls into his face. Damn, he's fine, and probably straighter than a pole up a nun's butt in church.

"Doesn't mean it wouldn't be beautiful."

"True." He scratches at the marks on his arms.

"What are they?" I pretend not to scrutinize his forearms.

"Scars I think, but I'm not sure. Have you ever seen this symbol before?"

Now I do study his arm, intently, struggling to resist the urge to run my fingers over the lines in his skin.

"Nope. Sorry. Did you try searching online?"

"Spent half the night doing it. Didn't get anywhere." Running a hand through his hair, he rises and stretches. "Any chance of grabbing breakfast?"

"You bet." Although I'm not sure how much longer I can afford to pay for Crow and still hope to make MarsLife tuition.

Leaving Bear to chew on one of Dad's old army boots, Crow and I traipse into the diner. We've got the place to ourselves for a bit. Suds and Bob whir into action at the flick of a switch. Tim takes a little more coaxing and a slap on the back for its circuits to connect.

"Old tech." I retreat from the grill as the bot lights the gas. "But it works."

"Want me to take a look?"

"Knock yourself out." I power down Tim and step aside so Crow can study the bot. "I've tried rewiring it, but I think there's a bug in the software."

"I'll check it out." In no time at all, Crow's got his fingers stuck into Tim's wiring, stabbing at the control screen. I focus on making waffles.

"This thing is ancient. Manufactured in 2029." He gives a low whistle. "If you're not going to do the right thing and recycle it" —He tosses me a smirk— "then it could definitely do with a firmware upgrade, but this should help for now." He clips the safety panel back onto Tim's chest and switches him on. This time, there's no slapping required to get the bot to perform its programmed tasks.

"How'd you do that?"

"I just did." Crow wiggles his fingers. "I could fix it

properly if you wanted. Do some maintenance on the others, too, if you need it."

"Yeah?" An idea takes root. "Hey, maybe I could get you a job fixing things 'round here in exchange for the room and food. Temporarily, of course."

"That would be epic. Think your family would mind?"

"I can ask." And pray Dale says yes, else I'll have to find a few more truckers willing to pay me to get horizontal.

"Sweet, thanks."

Fifteen minutes later we're sitting at the bar with waffles soaked in syrup. I should be watching the bots, but I can't take my eyes off Crow as he licks cream off his lips and flicks the curls out of his eyes every other bite.

He catches me staring. "Something wrong?"

"Nothing, I…" I swallow a mouthful of coffee. "Just wondering if you've remembered anything yet."

"Been trying to." He nibbles on a crisp edge of dough. "Had some disturbing dreams, though. Not sure if they're memories or not."

"You want to talk about it?" A needling suspicion skewers my insides.

"Um…" He sets down his knife and fork. "I broke my brother's tablet. Anyway, my father found out, but my brother took the blame. I was hiding under the bed—" Crow pauses and I hold my breath. "I could hear the belt, could hear my brother trying not to cry…" He shakes his head. "More of a nightmare, isn't it?"

My nightmare every time I made a mistake. I'd hide under the bed while West got beat and even with my hands clamped over my ears, I could still hear the crack of the belt and Weston's whimpers. Things I try not to think about, things I wish could stay buried, that did stay buried while I was medicated. Or at least didn't make me feel like shit when they wriggled to the surface.

"What's weird is that the dream felt so real," Crow says.

"Yeah?" It's all I can manage around the knot in my throat.

"We were playing with LEGO bricks and the screen made this really sad crunching noise when it broke. His SchoolPro900 had this scuff mark on the back like it'd been dropped before. I even remember the awful smell of the carpet under my bed because…" He chews on his bottom lip and frowns. "Because I think I wet myself under there. Listening to my dad and—well, I guess it's enough to scare the piss out of a little kid."

There's no way it's a coincidence. No way two kids break their brother's tablet with LEGO bricks and have the same reaction when their dad finds out.

"Were you looking at pictures of Mars before the tablet broke?" I have to be sure. "Pictures of the colony?"

"Yes. How the hell did you guess that?" Crow turns his full attention on me, green eyes wide and searching my face.

"That wasn't a dream." My voice quavers, and I take a deep breath. "And it's not your memory."

"What do you mean?" He narrows his gaze.

"That happened. To me."

"Your dad beat your brother, too?"

"No." He doesn't get it. "I mean, I broke my brother's SchoolPro. We were watching videos of Mars and fooling around and I cracked the screen with LEGO blocks."

"But that's exactly how I dreamed it." Crow turns a sickening shade of gray. "So you're saying I'm dreaming *your* memories?"

"Maybe. Tell me another one."

"Um, okay." He pauses to consider. "There was one about a dog fight."

"I was eight years old with my father and brother. The white dog died."

"It can't be." He chews on his thumb. "This can't be happening." He shakes his head and buries his face in his hands. "So everything I thought about Dead Rock, about the answers being here was because of you, your memories inside my brain. How is this possible?"

"I think something happened the night you fell out of the sky."

"I am not an alien," Crow says with vehemence.

"Maybe not, but when you fell there was this surge of energy, a pulse or something, that knocked me out for a bit. Maybe that's when we got all messed up and why we're sharing memories."

"Sharing memories?" He presses his palms flat against the counter. "You've been seeing my memories and never said anything?"

"I didn't know what I was seeing. How could I? I thought they were just really vivid dreams." Although I might've suspected. If I'm honest with myself, maybe I always knew the thoughts didn't belong to me, feeling like a favorite sweater that got shrunk in the dryer.

"Tell me something you've seen," Crow says.

"There was this one where I—you, I guess—won an academic award. Ring any bells?"

"I don't know." He taps his fork against the plate. "You remember anything else?"

"There was one about the ocean maybe, being on the beach."

"Anything more specific? Color of the sand, something to hint at location?"

"Brown sand. Blue sea." I shrug. "Postcard perfect."

"So it could've been Hawaii or Bali." He presses his thumbs against his eyebrows and closes his eyes. "Why is this happening?"

"Wish I knew." And more than that, I wish I knew how to

stop it before Crow sees something he shouldn't, something that'll change his opinion of me.

"We're sharing memories." Crow looks at me in bewilderment. "I mean, we are, right? It feels like I'm losing my mind."

"Yeah, me, too." And it makes me feel sick. There's a whole heap of stuff I don't want anyone to know, least of all some stranger I picked up in the desert.

"As cool as this could be on an existential level, it's also freaking me the fuck out. Who the hell am I, and how did I end up in Dead Rock?"

"I guess I'll be remembering for you." A thought as exciting as it is nauseating.

"You could end up knowing things about me I don't even know about myself." He chews on his lip. "I'm sure Baudrillard or Deleuze has a word for what we're experiencing."

"I'd prefer not living in a philosophical paradigm." It's too early to get into postmodern metaphysics. "What did Deleuze say about the self, something about it being a threshold, a door, and a becoming between two multiplicities, right? Think that's what's happening to us?"

"You can quote Deleuze?" Crow stares at me like I've sprouted a second head.

"What, because rednecks can't read, right?" Given my football free afternoons in juvie, I spent a heck of a lot of time in the library in the psychology and philosophy section trying to understand myself.

"I didn't mean it like that."

"Forget it. I'm used to it." Wait 'til I get to prove myself in those aptitude tests. Then it won't matter that my accent's thicker than a clump of blackjacks.

"I'm sorry, Raleigh." His apology sounds sincere.

"Forget it. Just don't go thinking I like the idea of you stumbling through my memories." If there's a way to block him from seeing inside my head, I've got to figure it out.

"This is so messed up." Crow folds his arms. "Unrestricted access to a person's memories, that's like rape of the mind."

"I know, but—" Our conversation is cut short by the chime of the opening door.

"Hiya, Raw." Abigail breezes through the diner, sashays over to us and gives me a hug, leaving an arm draped across my shoulders.

When I was five, I thought I'd marry this girl. By the time we were fourteen, she was in love with Weston, and I was in love with the Dead Rock Rattlers' running back. Wayne. I don't want to think about him. I can't. God, I hope Crow doesn't witness those moments of my life, not ever.

"Who's your friend?" She gives Crow the once over. So far, Crow's preferred to stay out of sight, and I haven't mentioned him to anyone except Madison.

"I'm Crow." He offers her his hand and I watch, half-expecting Abi to get a shock of images on contact.

"I'm Abi," she says with no sign of a brain assault. "Raw must really like you. He hasn't made me waffles since I grew boobs." She pouts and Crow chuckles while I'm char-grilled by embarrassment.

"They're delicious. The waffles, I mean." Crow smiles at me and the heat shifts from my face to my lower belly.

"Aw, listen to that." Abi's eyes—blue and orange today to match her fingernails—flash with interest, her gaze lingering on the scars on Crow's arms. "What's a fella like you doing in a place like this?"

"Sorry?" Crow raises a single eyebrow.

"You ain't hardly Texan. Where're you from?" She gives him the smile that melts the heart of almost every customer. I expect Crow to lean closer, to bask in the radiance of Abi's glow, for his gaze to rake down her body, but he looks at me instead.

"Just passing through." His knee nudges mine beneath the table.

"He was doing the historic sixty-six, but his car broke down." My mouth runs away with me, and before I have time to reconsider, Abi swallows the lie.

"I'm stranded here while I sort out details with the car hire company," Crow adds.

"That blows. Gotta go all the way to Amarillo I bet?"

"Looks like it."

"Well y'all enjoy your breakfast while I sort things in back." Throwing me a wink, Abi disappears into Dale's office.

Crow ignores the last few bites of waffle and nurses his coffee instead. "About figuring out who I am." He lowers his voice. "No one fitting my description has been reported missing in Texas or any of the neighboring states. It'll take a while to look through the rest of the U.S."

I nod and finish off the dregs in my mug.

"But I think I've got a better idea. What time do you get off today?" He slips his arms into his overalls as the man from 206 oozes into the diner. 206 throws me a nicotine-stained smile and my stomach struggles to hold onto the waffles. By the look on his face he'll be expecting my company again.

"If I can get Abi's brother to cover for me, maybe three." I turn my attention back to Crow.

"Meet me at my room then? And bring a camera." He winces as he stands, pressing the heel of his hand against his forehead.

"Headache?"

"Like a grenade going off inside my skull." He grimaces and a few moments later, he shakes his head. "It's gone now."

"I've been getting them, too, when I remember stuff."

"This is really happening, isn't it?" Crow frowns and bites his lip.

"Guess so."

"See you later?"

I nod and Crow departs, ignoring 206 and his leering gaze. I gather up our plates and head to the kitchen, but 206 beckons me with two hooked fingers. Reluctantly, I saunter over, trying my best to look nonchalant.

"What can I get ya?"

"Some more of what I got last time." He smirks and slides his hand onto his crotch. It would only take a second to drop the plates, grab the fork, and jam it into the guy's eye. Or maybe I go straight for what he values most and drive the tines right through his nuts. Fact is, I need the money now more than ever. Dale better agree to Crow helping out or I can kiss my Mars money goodbye, the one shot I have of getting out of this dump and far away from creeps like 206.

"It'll cost you more."

"You were worth every penny. How much?" He rubs his crotch, his gaze fixed on my chest. Now I regret wearing the too-tight shirt.

"Eleven-fifty."

"Ten-eighty." His other hand inches across the table, his fingers brushing the inside of my wrist.

"Eleven hundred."

"Done." A greasy smile spreads across his lips and bile tsunamis up my throat.

"See you tonight around ten," he says.

I retreat to the kitchen, my pride a shriveled carcass. Maybe it wouldn't be so bad being Crow, not knowing who you are or what you've done. God knows there's a lot about my life I wish I could forget or pretend never happened at all. Only hope those memories are buried deep enough that Crow won't ever see them.

"So, tell me 'bout this fella," Abi says with a sly smile.

"Nothin' to tell." I slam the dishes in the sink, and Suds gets to work with scrubbing brush appendages.

"He's cute."

"It's not like that."

"Sure it ain't." She twists a lock of blonde hair around her neon fingernail.

"You think your brother could cover for me this afternoon?"

"I knew it." Her solar flare smile is irresistible, and my lips quirk up into a grin despite the nausea in my belly.

"Just need time off, is all."

"I'll text Ford now." She whips the phone out of her bra and starts tapping at the screen. A few seconds later, it vibrates in her hand and her grin widens. "He says sure thing."

"Thanks."

"But, Raw." Her smile falters. "If he's just passing through…"

"I know." No matter who Crow is, when he eventually figures it out, the chances of him staying in Dead Rock are next to nothing.

"I don't wanna see you get hurt." She gives my arm a squeeze. "Now, tell me something *chido* 'bout Mars."

"According to the Darian calendar—" But I don't get too far before a man and a woman dressed in expensive suits settle in a booth at the window. The woman has her dark hair cropped close to her head soldier style.

"Tell me later." Abi grabs two eMenus and sets the day's special before scampering over to the newcomers. There's something about them that's intimidating, something almost military about the way they sit so straight, trying to look casual when they're both wound tighter than a guitar string. Feds, maybe, on their way up to the Coyote Creek supermax. Whoever they are, I hope they're just passing through.

"What happened to Tim?" Dale brandishes his egg flipper at the bot not turning the steaks into charcoal. "How'd you get it working?"

"There's this guy staying at the motel." My mouth is dry, but I force the words out anyway. "He fixed Tim."

"Oh yeah?" Dale raises a skeptical eyebrow.

"Yeah, he's got car problems. Waiting on a rental from Amarillo. Until then he kinda needs a job."

"I'll bet." Dale leans against the counter watching the bot work. "Sure did a bang up job."

"He doesn't want money, just to stay in the motel and eat in the diner 'til his ride gets sorted." I bash Suds who's got a lame elbow and is busy dousing the floor with soap bubbles. "We sure could use the maintenance on these."

"What kinda guy?" Dale asks.

"My age. Clean looking." I shrug. "He could do some other maintenance, too, if you wanted."

"So you don't have to." Dale's lips curl up in a knowing grin.

"So I can make more jewelry. Last lot sold for almost five hundred bucks."

"That's what I'm talking about. You could do some kind of training and become a— What do they call people who make jewelry?"

"Goldsmiths. So I'd become a what, a bonesmith?"

"Beats dishwasher, right?" Dale folds his arms. "Fine. This kid can stay as long as there's stuff needs fixin'. And you make sure he's not eating my prime rib every day."

"I'll tell him." It's hard to hide the smile tugging on my lips. Crow can stay and it won't cost me another penny.

At 2:57 p.m., Ford saunters into the kitchen while Dale's in the can.

"It's double on Sundays." He helps himself to a slice of cheese from the line.

"I wish. You're lucky I'm paying you at all."

"You going out for some—" Ford coordinates his tongue and hand in a terrible imitation of fellatio. "Abi told me about your boyfriend."

"She talks too much." No way a guy like Crow would want to be with a guy like me, not when he finds out how I can afford to pay his motel fees. A guy like Crow? The snapshot memories aren't exactly his life story. Maybe I've got nothing to worry about. He might've been in the system, too, and could have a rap sheet worse than mine. Not that I can imagine an award-winning kid like that in trouble with the law.

"So, no eating crow today?" He jabs me in the ribs with his elbow. My face burns hotter than the sun and words desert me.

"See you 'round, Raw." He chuckles. "Have fun. Be safe." Ford likes to pretend he's my big brother even though he's only eleven months older than Abi and me.

I slip out of the kitchen with a burrito wrapped up to go before Dale can argue, but Madison sees me from the store window and catches me in the parking lot.

"Hey, Leigh, we gotta talk." She strides over with Nash perched on her hip. "What's this about the drifter we found working at my diner?" She snaps a gum bubble and raises her eyebrows.

"Did you tell Dale about how we found him?"

"You're still wearing your skin, aren't you?"

"Thanks, I guess."

"You're welcome," she says. "Now start talking."

"It's complicated."

"No, it's not." Her eyes flash with anger just like our father's. At least Maddy's temper is more a long simmer and less an instant volcano. "We don't know the fella, and now he's working around the place, around my son. He should be long gone by now."

"Crow's a good guy. He just needs some time to sort things out."

"What things, Leigh?" Her eyes are lasers. "Where's he from and what was he doing laying out in the middle of nowhere like that. Is it drugs?"

"Hell, no."

"What then?"

"Trust me, he won't be a problem. He'll be gone soon, promise." Far sooner than I'm probably going to like.

"I do trust you." Madison swings Nash to her other hip. "I always have and look where it's got me."

"That's real nice of you."

"Hey." She catches my arm before I can storm off in my cloud of indignation. "I've got a kid to think of. I don't want any trouble is all." She sighs and releases my wrist. "I don't want you going and getting yourself mixed up in anything."

"It's not like that." Would everyone stop seeing things that aren't there already?

"He told you what happened, who bust him up?"

"He can't remember."

"Raleigh!" Madison throws her free hand in the air and shakes her head.

"It's true. Some kind of amnesia." No point trying to tell her we're sharing memories. It'll only send Madison over the edge and get Crow and I both committed.

"Ain't that mighty convenient."

"Look, what I do know about Crow, he seems like a stand-up guy in a spot of trouble. Ain't helping him the Christian thing to do?"

"Don't go using the God you've never believed in against me." Frown lines gather like a thunderstorm on her forehead. She looks so much like my dad I half expect her to take a swing at me. "You're so close to getting out of here," she says. "Whether it's Mars or somewhere else. Don't throw that away over some pretty boy with a sob story. You're better than that, Leigh."

"I'll be careful."

"You better be. If I suspect trouble, I'll call Sheriff Daniels myself. Got it?"

"Thanks, Maddy." I give her a kiss on the cheek and tousle Nash's hair before she can continue the tirade.

Seconds later, I knock on 204. Crow answers. Shirtless. My mouth turns dry as Mars as I step across the threshold.

CROW

"Don't you eat salad in Texas?" I ask as Raleigh hands me a burrito. What I wouldn't give for some romaine and prosciutto with a balsamic vinaigrette instead of half a tub of mayo.

"Not if I can help it. It's like chewing on crunchy water." Raleigh sounds like he's choking on the words, his gaze resting everywhere but on me. What's wrong with the guy?

"How do you stay in shape living on fast food?" My gaze rakes him up and down. The dude is fit, with broad shoulders and bulging biceps somehow incongruent with his long hair, but I like it. Actually… There's a tightening in my abs as I stare at Raleigh, appreciating his good looks and built body squeezed into the tight shirt. It's not the first time I've noticed, either. My pulse quickens and I stand a little taller, a stupid grin stretching across my face. I'm attracted to him. Holy mother of God, I'm *attracted* to him. Guess the body doesn't need the brain's cooperation to react to certain stimuli, and mine's reacting in spades. Is there a surreptitious way to rearrange my pants without Raleigh noticing? I slip my hand into my pocket and try to give myself a little more room, but it's not working.

"I…um…" He squirms.

"You played football." Best I sit down. It's like being a pubescent schoolkid all over again, trying to hide your surprise boner behind your desk and hoping no one notices.

"Another memory?" He looks worried.

"You on the field beneath the lights, the crowd going wild." They were calling his name, cheering for the QB who could read the defense like Rain Man could process numbers. He always found the opening, going for big plays that took the Rattler's all the way to state championships. "You were really good." And remembering Raleigh on the football field

isn't helping the situation south of my waist, which means…
I scrutinize Raleigh some more. The guy is hot, like I want to knot my fingers in his hair and let my tongue follow the hard outlines of his body so perfectly molded by his T-shirt kind of hot.

I'm gay. I mean, I must be. I am gay. A sense of truth, of rightness settles inside me, and I can't help but smile. Guess that's one more fact I can check off the list of stuff I needed to know about myself.

"I hated football," Raleigh says.

"That doesn't change how good you were."

He shrugs and seems to fold in on himself, avoiding eye contact.

"Have you seen any more about me?" I ask, my body starting to behave a little less like a horny teenager's.

"Not since the award thing. Any luck with the research?" He sits at the table while I dismantle the burrito and ferret out the healthier bits.

"There's still nothing at all about a meteor, or a man falling out the sky."

"Yeah, I looked, too. There isn't even hokey speculation about UFOs. It's like that night in the desert never even happened." He frowns.

"Conspicuous by its absence, maybe?"

"You're sitting right in front of me so we know you're real, regardless of what the 'net does or doesn't say. Or do you want to start quoting Lacan?" A smirk creeps across his lips.

"It's not a competition, you know. I don't mind you being smarter than me." It seems I underestimated this guy, which only makes him all the more intriguing.

"I doubt I am," he says.

"We'll see." I gaze at him, studying his dark eyes and the way his hair frames his square jaw. I want to kiss him with an urgency that's both exhilarating and terrifying, but would he let me?

"I've got some good news." He breaks the moment of tense silence. "Dale was impressed with how Tim was running. He said you can stay as long as there's stuff to fix."

"For real?" That's a relief, not that I imagine I'll be making this crappy little town my home any time soon.

"Don't get too excited. Ain't going to be fun."

"When do I start?"

"Tomorrow."

"Thanks. For everything." I knock over the open water bottle, and we both try to catch it, our fingers meeting as we grab the plastic. The contact feels like getting zapped by lightning. There's a jolt down my spine and we spring apart, all the hair on our arms standing up.

Images flood my mind: *fists in my face, my nose bleeding, blood in my eye. Despite that I struggle to my feet and lash out, enjoying the sound of a nose breaking. More football, tackling a guy and gazing into his ice blue eyes. A rotund woman I call Mama crying her eyes out at the kitchen table. Running through the scrub with Bear at my heels.*

"Damn, that was intense." Like trying to hug a Van der Graaff generator. "Did you see something?"

Raleigh nods and takes a moment to compose himself before answering. "You stood on a soldering iron despite your mom telling you not to work in the garage barefoot. More of the ocean and I think you were at school, some fancy Ivy League place all red brick buildings and guys playing hacky sack on the lawn. You were studying in a library—physics, I think."

A soldering iron. My foot itches. Studying physics in the library at… The memories don't seem right. Something doesn't fit.

```
tech1@cer-ro:~$ cd /home/core2
tech1@cer-ro:~$ restore *.mem
```

I squeeze my eyes shut, letting the memories settle over me, puzzle pieces slotting into place.

"What did you see?" Raleigh starts tearing up the edges of the burrito wrapping.

"You getting into fights, some guy with blue eyes, and you taking Bear for a run." I pause, gauging his reaction. He nods and I continue. "I also saw your mom crying at the kitchen table."

"She did that a lot after Weston died."

"I'm sure she wasn't the only one." After a moment, I continue. "When you see things, do you only see them, or..." I'm going to sound like a lunatic for asking this. "Do you like, feel things, too?"

"Like what?"

"Like I felt how much—" It feels like an invasion of what little privacy we have left to mention this, but it's not like I can unsee Raleigh's memory. "I know you liked the guy with blue eyes, and I felt how much it hurt to see your mom crying." I also felt his joy at being able to fight back, his satisfaction as his attacker's nose broke, and his elation running wild through the scrub.

"Oh." He studies his hands. "I guess I feel things, too, like how proud you were winning that award or how much you hated campus coffee. Also, that hearing your mom say 'I told you so' hurt you more than the missing skin on your foot."

"Good to know." I smile and Raleigh returns the gesture, renewing my desire to kiss him.

"You said you had an idea?" he asks.

"I do." Oh so very many, but I bite my tongue. "Image

recognition. I was thinking we could take a photo of these symbols and see if we get any hits online. What do you think?"

"Should've thought about it sooner." He takes his phone out. "Do you think the scars mean something?"

"They're definitely not random. I must've gone through a fuck-ton of pain for these, and it's the same symbol over and over." My hand coasts across my chest, resting above the intricate spiral carved into my solar plexus. The keloid here isn't as bubbly as a regular scar, but rather like the pattern has been woven through my flesh. A high-end body mod.

"You think you got this done, like scarification?" Raleigh's eyes widen.

"I was thinking more like a ritualistic cult thing, but yeah, I guess scarification is a possibility, too." I wink and Raleigh almost laughs. It must be really nice to see his face light up. Most of the time he looks pensive, like he's part Atlas, part Prometheus.

"Do you think it could be like a map?" His gaze slips down my body, following the scars where they disappear beneath the waist band of the overalls.

"Maybe. I guess you'll have to follow where they lead." The scars are etched over my hips and continue along my thighs. Raleigh looks at me like he's imagining me wearing only the scars, and I love it.

"They must be important." His Adam's apple bobs when he swallows. He seems unable to tear his gaze off my body, and I love that, too.

"No one gets shredded like this purely for aesthetics."

"Want me to start shooting?" His gaze meets mine.

"Let's get one of my face, obviously." I stand up. "And then maybe the one on my chest?" I tap the spot between my pecs.

Raleigh nods and fumbles with the phone before snapping one of my face. Taking a step closer, he snaps another of my chest. He smells of spicy musk and dust—a not unpleasant fragrance—but he's careful not to touch me.

"There's more on my back, too." The engravings tumble down my spine to my coccyx. It must've taken hours to get this done and a boatload of cash.

Raleigh's hand hovers above my flesh, a static charge tickling the fine hairs on my back as he snaps another photo. Christ, I wish he'd touch me already.

"These are amazing." His breath wafts across my skin and sets every nerve on fire. Is it weird that I want him to touch me so bad? I do. Not because I want the whiplash of a memory storm, but because I want to feel his hands on me. My blood pressure spikes as he inches even closer.

"Thank you." My voice is more of a croak than the sexy huskiness I was hoping for.

"For what?" Raleigh looks at me with eyes I could drown in.

"If it weren't for you, I'd still be bleeding in the middle of nowhere."

"I just did what any decent person would." Raleigh clears his throat and puts some distance between us. "I can edit these on my computer." He heads for the door.

"Can I come?" I pull on my shirt, which takes monumental effort when all I really want to do is shed the rest of my clothes with this guy.

After some hesitation, he nods and holds open the door for me. I step across the threshold and hear the voices again.

"He shouldn't be able to control the 'scape this way. Is there a bug in the program?"

What 'scape?

"Did you hear something?" I ask.

"Like what?" Raleigh frowns. A semi blows its horn on the interstate, and cars pull in and out of the station. Despite the ruckus around me, the voices persist.

"No bug," the voice says. **"We built this program to be manipulated. It's just we haven't ever seen such a strong response in a candidate. The sero is getting owned."**

Sero?

"Not a good thing," another voice interjects.

"Not a bad thing, either."

"Is it safe to continue?"

"I'll run the updated version. Might give us a bit more control."

"Crow, are you all right?" Raleigh asks. "You look kinda pale."

"I'm fine." I'm definitely not, but at least the voices fade as I follow Raleigh up to the house. I could've been imagining it, might be having a psychotic break—or maybe I've escaped from the loony bin—but how could I imagine words I don't even understand?

```
tech1@cer-ro:~$ reboot
tech1@cer-ro:~$ chmod +x psytek-2.14.10 && ./
psytek-2.14.10
```

Raleigh

If Crow knew what I'd done, knew what I planned on doing later tonight, he wouldn't want to be anywhere near me. I hope he never gets to see those memories.

Inhale. My heart slams juggernaut blows against my ribs. *Exhale.* I need to run, to clear my head, an endorphin rush. How do I stay in shape living on Dale's food? I run. One day, I might keep running right on down the interstate and never come back. But not now. Now I've got Crow trailing after me.

"Wow, sweet." Crow strides across my room to the aquarium. "I've never seen one like this before." He traces the journey of a bloodfin tetra as it swims from bowl to bowl along the convoluted tubing. "Did you make all those?" He points at a cave structure replete with castle turrets.

"Took four jackrabbits to make that one."

"Dude, you're an artist. Seriously."

"It's fish tank decor."

"Doesn't make it any less impressive." He slides to the floor and leans against my bed, the glow from the aquarium casting MC Escher shadows across his face.

"I doubt it'll make me a billionaire."

"Is that what you want?" He straightens his legs and folds his hands in his lap. I grab the tablet off my desk and connect it to my phone before settling opposite him with my back against the bookcase.

"I just need enough for MarsLife."

"Hence the posters." He looks around my room, and his gaze settles on the poster of Deshaun Brown, the fourth person to set foot on Mars. "What's so special about Brown?"

"There was tons of controversy when MarsLife announced he'd be one of the first astronauts going up. He came from the ghettos, and no one thought he'd amount to much, but he worked hard and he did it. Highest scoring cadet in his class and he went to Mars." And if he can do it, then maybe I can, too.

"Why MarsLife? Why not college?" Crow asks.

"MarsLife doesn't care about your past. They're focused on the future, looking for the best and brightest to pave the way for the rest of humanity. They're holding open aptitude tests next month. If I can get the tuition together and pass the test, I might actually get to leave this dump." *If if if...* Too many variables. Too much riding on somebody else's opinion of me.

"You want to be an astronaut?" Crow raises a single eyebrow.

"Since I was six years old."

"And you're set on Mars?"

"The moon is boring." An artificial paradise for the insanely rich. "Mars is the new frontier. The possibilities there are endless." A new world, a new life, a new me.

"Seems more like a radiation-burned wasteland."

"How would you know?" The dream-memory of the stasis habitat looms in my mind. Crow might know a heck of a lot more about Mars than he realizes.

"I guess I don't." He shrugs. "I just think Earth's got a lot to offer."

"But for how much longer? We've pretty much guaranteed our own self-destruction."

"And our answer is to do more of the same only on a different planet?" The hint of bitterness in his tone doesn't quite match the wry grin on his face.

"I'd like to believe we can do better. That there's hope for humanity. Maybe this time we'll get it right."

"With people like you on Mars, I'm sure we will." His words settle over me like a warm blanket on a cold night. "Hey, have you got the complete Herbert collection?" He nods his head toward my bookcase stacked with vintage paperbacks from Asimov and Dick, Sagan, Hubert, and Hubbard.

"Yeah, although nothing beats the original."

"I agree." Crow cocks his head to the side. "*Whether a thought is spoken or not, it is a real thing and has powers of reality.*"

"You remember obscure quotes from a seventy-year-old novel, but not your own name?"

"Apparently." He frowns.

"Running an image search might take a while." The search bar inches in micro increments toward completion as the app analyzes the picture of his face before trying to find matches online.

"Not like I've got to be somewhere else." Crow's fingers splay across his chest, resting above the spiral carved into his sternum. The symbols are strange, almost as if he were born with them. Birthmarks, not scars.

"So what do these MarsLife aptitude tests involve?" he asks.

"Three-tier. Physical first, then mental acuity tests, and the last is a psychological evaluation to make sure you don't go nuts and murder your crew." It's the third test I'm most concerned about. I upload a couple images of his scars, giving me an excuse not to look at him.

"Is murder a possibility?"

"It happened on the Endeavour III. A woman went stir-crazy and axed a fellow crew member before the rest of the crew could knock her out. That's why the new screening process is so thorough." And expensive for candidates.

"Sounds intense."

"It is." I chew on my lip. I have to tell him. That memory could be the key to who he is. "The first night after I found you, I had a dream. Well, I thought it was a dream then." I take a deep breath. "You were in a sim for the habitat module of an interplanetary cruiser prepping for cryo-stasis.'"

"What does that mean exactly?" Crow leans forward.

"It means you were training to be an astronaut. That you might've been assigned to a Mars mission."

"That's crazy." He tugs his hand through his hair. "Maybe you remember wrong?"

"Been right so far, haven't I?"

"So you think I went on a Mars mission and took a tumble out of the sky?"

"Being an astronaut is better than being an alien, right?"

"Although not exactly more plausible." He presses the heels of his hands against his eyes, seeming to smear dark circles beneath them.

"It's kinda *chido,* you being en route to Mars." There's no stopping the slow grin stretching across my lips. Crow regards me for several long moments, the frown cemented on his face.

"I was in training. A sim. Let's not jump to intergalactic conclusions. Besides," he says, "if I was going to Mars, how am I here?"

"Emergency ejection?"

Hugging his knees to his chest, he chuckles bitterly. "And how do you explain surviving re-entry?"

"No idea. I'm outta theories." The app beeps in completion and starts searching for online matches.

"Do you know which mission that might've been?" Frown lines cut canyons across his forehead.

I jab at the tablet, searching through the MarsLife website for crew information. Endeavor I, Entropy I and II, Endeavor II and III… There are over three hundred names on the official lists, names without faces. But there are photos of the crew. I've seen entire Pin-it reels dedicated to the astronauts and Martian colonizers, brave adventurers who set out undaunted by the perils of space.

"There!" A photo taken for New Scientific Earth of the

Entropy II crew. "That's you." I enlarge the image and show Crow the tablet. He scoots over so that we're sitting next to each other, careful not to touch.

"That's a blurry pixel." He studies the image.

"That's definitely you." Crow went to Mars—or was at least on his way there. I'm sitting next to an astronaut! Excitement bubbles up through my insides like a Mentos in a Coke bottle.

"Could be anyone," he says. We both read the names and professions listed beneath the photo: engineers, geologists, you name it, until he reaches third from the left in the back row.

"B. Cozens, software specialist, Bennett Institute." Crow's hands are shaking as he zooms in on the photo. There's a weird expression on his face.

"Ringing a bell this time?" I ask.

"It's really hard to say. It's like part of me recognizes the name…" His eyes roll back in his head, and I catch him before he hits the floor.

"Crow?"

He mumbles something incoherent and his eyes swivel back into normal position. I glimpse a flash of purple in his eyes, but he blinks and it's gone. Two perfectly green marbles stare up at me.

"You okay?"

"Did I faint?"

"I think so."

He groans and holds his head. We should really get to a hospital. A concussion might be the least of his problems, and I say as much.

"Not yet. Not until I know more."

"We can start with the Bennett Institute." I look it up. A research facility specializing in space tech. Their logo is a stylized spiral galaxy exactly like the one etched all over Crow.

"Holy shit, that's my symbol." Crow points at the screen and tugs up his shirt, revealing the scar carved into his sternum. "I mean, it is, right?"

"Totally." The symbols are identical. He has a spiral galaxy carved repeatedly into his flesh. If I didn't think he could be an alien before, I certainly do now. A million thoughts ricochet inside my skull, a million colliding possibilities.

"If I got this institute's logo cut into me so many times, this place must be important."

"It's where you must've been working, and loving it I guess, to turn yourself into a walking advertisement."

"This is insane." He lowers his T-shirt and scrutinizes the symbols on his arms, the same spiral rendered over and over.

"Working at Bennett—loyalty to the company aside— makes sense since they design space tech and I'm pretty sure you went to Mars."

"Raleigh," Crow interjects. "There's no flipping way I went to Mars. You know why? Because that guy in the picture isn't me and even if he was, he went to Mars two years ago. *Mars.* He's on a different planet, and I'm here."

"But I saw you on the ship."

"In a simulation! I didn't plummet from outer space." His laughter is sardonic. "And even if I was jettisoned by a spacecraft, there's no way I'd survive a fall to the ground. It's not possible."

"Like our memory share isn't possible?"

That shuts him up, leaving his mouth opening and closing on non-existent words. My tablet chirrups and I open the notification. Zero matches for Crow's face. I was so sure the guy in the photo was him, but my app thinks differently.

"Odd." I re-run the analysis. Maybe it's a malfunction in the software.

"Why's that odd?"

"Who our age isn't on social media?"

"I told you that wasn't me." Crow sounds both relieved and dejected.

"Not finding a single match is impossible." I try again, this time including "B. Cozens" and "Bennett Institute" in the search. Still nothing. "Seems like someone went to a lot of trouble to make sure you couldn't be found."

"Or make it seem like I never existed at all." Crow's expression darkens. "Maybe I don't exist. Maybe…"

Another flash of purple in his eyes. This time I didn't imagine it. He zones out for a moment, his irises shaking back and forth like he's having a seizure. He blinks and sighs.

A dozen possibilities race through my mind, each lifted from sci-fi thrillers. Maybe Crow was right bringing up Baudrillard. Considering how far immersion gaming has come, I'm not sure how we'd tell if we were in a virtual reality without a computer controlling the duration of the trip. That feels an awful lot like wish fulfillment. No way my life in Dead Rock isn't real. No virtual reality would be this bleak.

Crow might not be an alien, but that doesn't mean he's human. Android technology is advancing all the time. Maybe he's a military experiment gone wrong and dumped like trash— I stop myself from finishing the thought. Without the meds, my imagination sure can run away with me.

"What are you thinking?" I say.

"I don't know." He runs a hand through his hair, letting the curls fall disheveled over his ears. "Okay, tell me what you saw that night. In detail."

I do, recounting every moment in the scrub.

"And you're sure you hadn't been drinking?" he asks.

"You think I'm making it up?"

"No, man, just that this is so whack."

"I still reckon this Bennett Institute is our best bet. According to the website it's in Nebraska." As is the Offutt airbase, home of the United States Strategic Command and

HQ of the MarsLife Corps.

"Too bad there's no email address or phone number." Crow hits tab after tab without finding any contact information. That's odd all by itself.

"I'll poke around the Web some more and see if I can find an address." There's a hollow ache in the pit of my stomach, a creeping emptiness that seeps into my veins. Soon as Crow finds out who he is, he'll hightail it out of Dead Rock, and I'll bet he won't look back, especially not if he's destined for Mars. *Mars.* Can't help thinking maybe Mars could be in the cards for both of us. Brown did it against the odds, and so will I. For West, for myself, and maybe for Crow as well.

"I hope they've got answers for me." Crow scrunches his eyes closed, then opens them again and squints. "My eyes are killing me." He rubs them aggressively.

"Probably got dust in them."

"Feels like the whole damn Chihauhaun desert. Can you take a look?"

Holding my breath, I peer into his face and confirm my suspicions. His eyes are green with veins of purple running through the irises.

"Nothing." Crow might think I'm crazier than a sprayed roach if I mention anything about my theories on advanced robotics.

"I need to remember, Raleigh." He takes my hand and the familiar crackle of electricity sparks between us. My mind rips away.

We've been hiking for hours, trekking along the Panorama trail. Dad tosses me a water bottle, and I squirt as much over my head as I do down my throat. It's hot, the California sun cutting through wispy clouds.

"*Careful*," *Dad says, pushing me up the slope. I'm eleven and I am not afraid, not with my dad right behind me, keeping up a constant stream of encouragement. When we reach the top, he hugs me and musses my hair.*

"*Good job, kiddo.*" *There's pride in his voice.*

The switchback is flat on top, a plateau that stretches toward Nevada. Dad picks up a stone and tosses it out into the air.

"*One-one-thousand, two-one-thousand…*" *I count off the seconds, imagining what it might be like to be that pebble dropping through the air.*

After another couple of hours hiking up and down steep switchbacks, storm clouds broil in the distance, and we head down to Curry Village. Dad's all smiles and love and gentle hands and when I grow up I want to be just like him.

CROW

Raleigh's scars are soft beneath my fingertips, soft and pliable the way scars should be. The static charge pulses up my arms and a memory plays out in my mind like a snippet from a film, except I'm not just watching it, I'm living it, feeling every moment.

The razor blade is tricky to hold, but I brace my hand against the rim of the basin and draw the first lines across my skin. This pain is nothing compared to what West experienced, the pain that eventually drove him head-on into that rig. The blade sinks into my skin and blood fills the basin in dark ribbons as I carve West's memory into my flesh.

"Raleigh!" Madison rushes into the bathroom and slaps the blade from my hand. She grabs fresh white towels and wraps them around my wrists. Her face is pale, her eyes wide and bloodshot from crying. She slaps me hard across the face.

"What the hell do you think you're doing?"

"It's Comanche tradition." I shrug, despite my heart fixin' to burst out of my chest. "When someone dies, you show your pain." I'm not trying to kill myself. I don't want to die.

Madison's eyes fill once more with tears and she hugs me, crushing me while she sobs. After a moment, I realize she's not holding me so much as I'm holding her.

"I can't lose you, too, Leigh. Promise me." She chokes out the words, but it's a promise I can't make, not when I promised West I'd go to Mars.

I release Raleigh's hands, and we sit in contemplative silence for several long moments, both digesting what we saw of each oth-er's life. So the woman who tried to pay me to leave is Raleigh's sister. It makes sense now, her wanting me away from him. She was just being the protective big sister she's always been.

"You're Comanche?" I ask.

"A quarter." There's pride in his voice. "Not that my father ever let us have much to do with that side of the family. Most of what I know I read online."

"You weren't trying to kill yourself." I ghost my thumb across the scars cut all the way around his wrists.

"I'd never do that. Not after West," he says. "According to some sources, it was the women who cut themselves, but cutting only my hair didn't seem enough."

Goose bumps erupt across my skin, every single hair on my body standing at attention. I could kiss him. He's so close and his bottom lip trembles just a little.

"Are you okay?"

"I'm terrified," he says. "Terrified of you finding out something I don't want you to."

"Don't be." *He's* afraid? He's got a front row seat to things I can't remember. I'm the one who should be a nervous wreck. "What did you see about me?"

"You were hiking in Yosemite with your dad."

I scratch at the stubble dusting my jaw. "Think I'm from California?"

"Maybe. You're not from the south."

"Were we on the Panorama trail?" The memory slithers into my mind, filling up a void.

"Maybe. You know, my dad always promised to take us hiking out there." Raleigh sounds wistful.

"He didn't?" Fuck, my eyes hurt! My vision distorts, the periphery crumbling like a dried-out cookie.

"The military was his real family," Raleigh says and the sadness in his voice makes me want to hug him. "You starting to remember more on your own?" he asks.

"Every time you catch a glimpse of my life, it somehow blows back on me. It's like you're a conduit for my memories."

The memories are more like half-remembered dreams, except the bit about Mars. Which means what? That I went to Mars, that I was en route to the planet at least. Maybe something happened to the cruiser and we had to evacuate. Then our escape pod failed and I got tossed into the desert. It doesn't seem totally impossible, but then there would've been media coverage and a rescue mission and I wouldn't have been found butt naked by Raleigh. The more I think about it, the more I'm forced to face the fact that desert-arrival courtesy of an escape pod is highly unlikely, which whittles down the options to improbable and straight up bizarre.

"Hey, I've got to run some errands," Raleigh says. "Think we could call it a night?" He looks nervous as he gets to his feet with his arms folded across his chest.

"Of course. And thanks, man." I hesitate in the doorway. "We'll figure this out. One way or another."

"I know." He ushers me past the kitchen where Madison and Dale are preparing dinner. Dale frowns at us; Madison looks concerned, her lips pressed into a tight line. I give her a nod, hoping it's enough to allay her fears. If they only knew the half of it. As it is they must be pretty cool to let a stranger live off their goodwill.

"I'll see you tomorrow?" I ask Raleigh when we reach the porch.

"My shift starts at eight."

"Good night then." Again, a moment of awkwardness as our eyes meet. The tightness in my stomach and burning in my chest makes me want to kiss him. Maybe I've got it all wrong and he'll end up punching me in the face if I even tried, but there's a look in his eyes that makes me think he might kiss me back.

"Night." He shuts the screen door and disappears into the

house, leaving me alone with the stars and ineffable emotions.

With Bear at my heels, I trudge down to the motel. B. Cozens, B. Cozens—I play the name on repeat in my head until the words lose all meaning. Semantic satiation. I can remember that useless fact, but not my own freaking name. Bear follows me into the motel room and rolls onto his back for belly rubs. Kicking off my shoes, I settle on the bed to access the touchscreen, rubbing my bare feet across Bear's tummy.

B. Cozens. Bennett Institute. The search yields no results. Aside from the single Entropy crew image, there doesn't appear to be any record of me. It truly is like I don't exist, like I never existed at all.

Shooting pain in my eyes drives me into the bathroom, and I peer into the mirror. My eyes flash purple and the voices return.

"The program isn't supposed to be cognizant." The speaker is irritated.

"I'm not doing it. It's all Williams." That voice sounds defensive.

"Shut it down. This isn't working."

"I disagree." A third voice, one I haven't heard before, enters the mix. **"I'd like to see how this progresses. Reboot when you have to, but let the 'scape play out. We wanted an advanced analysis and it looks like we're going to get it."**

"Want me to up the ante?" The familiar voice asks.

"Keep it in context, but yes, let's throw him a few curve balls."

The voices fade leaving me alone with my freaky eyes and turbulent thoughts.

What the fuck am I?

```
tech1@cer-ro:~$ chmod +x psytekextras-2.14.8 && ./
psytekextras-2.14.8
```

RALEIGH

Tying up my hair, I head down to 206. How long until Crow sees all the things I want to keep buried? Not that I have a choice. If it's my dignity or a shot at Mars, I guess it's gonna be Mars. The red planet seems less out of reach tonight, a brighter spot in the glowing constellations. It doesn't matter what it costs me now to get there. It'll be worth doing a hundred 206s if it means getting to Mars and getting to remake my life.

The door opens after a single knock and 206 smirks at me after glancing left and right over my shoulders.

"Come on in, son."

Taking a deep breath, I hold the image of Mars in my mind and step across the threshold, but the sound of splintering glass stops me mid-stride.

I leave 206 and sprint toward the ruckus at the gas station. Bear beat me to it.

"Ow, fuckin' mutt. Kill it, kill it!" Lilah Mulhoney yells. She's flailing amidst glass shards outside the station store with Bear locked onto her jeans. Vince swings his baseball bat, aiming at my dog's head.

"Hey!" I launch myself at Vince, trying to wrestle the bat out of his hands. We're in eighth grade again, my fists in his face, bashing the teeth from his skull. He's had more practice since then and manages to land a blow to my jaw. Fireworks explode across my vision. He takes another shot, but I'm faster and pummel his nose, the wet crunch of cartilage so satisfying. And just like that, I break my streak of good behavior.

Bear yelps as Lilah smacks him with the bat. She scrambles free and raises the bat again, this time aiming for me. Bear charges in and grabs her arm, shaking his head side to side. Lilah screams obscenities that would make a sailor blush. He'll rip her arm off, and for that, they'll kill my dog.

"Leave it!" I grab Bear by the collar, fending off one-armed blows from Lilah. She tries to hit my dog and ends up bashing me across the shoulders instead.

"Leave!" I put my face against his, staring down my pit. "Bear, let go." With a growl, he spits out Lilah's arm, hackles still raised and lips bloodied.

"Your dog almost ate my arm." Lilah cradles her damaged limb.

"You busted our windows." I point to the splinters littering the ground.

"I hope they turn that mutt into sausage meat," Vince mutters, his face a red fountain.

"What the hell is your problem?" I scream at Vince. If he'd left me alone in elementary school, I might never have hit him in the first place and avoided all of what followed after that schoolyard fight.

"You, *pendejo.*" He spits.

"If I catch you 'round here again, I'll kill you."

"Don't think you got the balls." Lilah sneers through the tears streaking her face. "Do you even have balls, squaw?"

My vision blurs. I pick up her discarded bat and go in swinging. A blow or two and her skull would shatter like an egg under a hammer, blood and brains spilling across asphalt. Vince backs away, leaving his sister defenseless. It would be so easy, just like last time, getting lost in the rhythm of smashing, a relentless motion fueled by hatred and rage and pain. But I'm not that person anymore. *You're better than this. You're better than them.* My hands tremble, the bat wobbling in my grip. I take a menacing step toward Lilah. Arms wrap around my own, pinning them down hard and leaving the bat dangling useless from my hands.

"You don't want to do this," Crow says, and electricity bolts through my bones.

I'm fifteen and taking off my underwear with a boy called Jeremy. My pulse quickens at the thought of being discovered, of Mom walking in on us. But Jeremy kisses me, obliterating every thought in my head.

"Let me go." I squirm, but his embrace is strong, impossibly strong. His arms don't give at all.

"Raleigh!" Crow spins us around, deflecting the blow Vince aimed at my head with his shoulder. The bat makes contact with a sickening crunch.

"What the fuck?" Vince stares at the splintered bat, his gaze shifting from me to Crow. Vince prepares for another attack, but the crack of a gunshot stops him in his tracks. We all duck for cover.

"That's enough, I reckon." The man from 206 brandishes his gun. The other guests have come out for the show, too, and the front door of the house slams open.

"His dog—" Lilah starts.

"You got what you were askin' for," 206 says. "Now get before I shoot your toes off."

"This ain't over, fuckhead," Vince yells over his shoulder as he and Lilah scramble into their pickup.

"You okay?" Crow presses his fingers to my face and a thrill of warmth worms its way through my veins. He drops his hand before more memories can assault us.

"I'll live." I spit up a gobbet of blood-frothed saliva and run my tongue along my lips tasting copper. "I've had worse." Severing our contact, I kneel down beside Bear and check him for injuries.

"Is he all right?" Crow asks.

"He's had worse, too." I give Bear a scratch under his chin, trying to avoid getting Lilah's blood licked all over my face. "Thanks, I guess." My gaze drifts to the splintered bat, the bat that should've done serious damage to Crow's shoulder.

"It's the least I could do." Crow shrugs.

"Raleigh!" Dale charges down the path from the house, his face turning red.

"Go." I jerk my head toward the motel. Crow hesitates. "You shouldn't get involved in this."

"I am involved."

"Please, Crow."

"Fine." He raises his hands and steps away, taking up with the other spectators.

"What the hell did you do?" Dale surveys the damage, the baseball bats, blood, and broken glass.

"I seen what happened," 206 says. "The boy here chased off the culprits."

"The Mulhoneys," I add.

"And did you sic your dog on them?" Dale's face is livid.

"Bear was just defending me, defending your property."

"Can't stay out of trouble, can you?" Dale glares at me with a mix of anger and disappointment.

"They were busting up your store." My hands ball into fists again, my own rage spitting and fizzing hot inside my chest.

"Then you shoulda called the cops." Dale shakes his head. "They report this, you're going away. You get that, right? You're not a kid anymore. This is permanent record stuff. Christ, Raleigh!" His face scrunches up with genuine concern.

"I'll vouch for the boy. He didn't do nothin' wrong."

"And who the hell are you?" Dale turns to 206.

"Buddy Mitchell." He holds out his hand to Dale and my guts twist into Twizzlers. It's easier not knowing their names, that way all the anonymous hookups bleed into a blur of memory that can be brushed aside. Soon as they have a name, I feel marked, branded, like I can never wash their presence off my skin.

"Dale Buckner. You a regular?"

"Pass through every few weeks."

"Well, sir. If you agree to vouch for Raleigh if it comes to it, then I think we can be a little more accommodating on the price of your room."

I crush window shards beneath my heels while Dale and Buddy Mitchell sort out the specifics.

"You." Dale points a finger at me. Buddy gives me a smirk over Dale's shoulder and bile rises up the back of my throat. He'll expect my services for free now. "Get this cleaned up," Dale barks as if I was the one breaking the windows in the first place.

"This wasn't my fault."

"Not your fault?" He stands real close to me. "I don't know what beef you got with the Mulhoneys, but this has got to stop. You think I don't remember what you did to Vince. Christ, Raleigh, what you did to his cousin? It's like you *want* to go to Coyote Creek." He shoves a finger in my chest, and I take a deep, shuddering breath to keep from snapping that finger right off his hand.

"You ever bother learning why I did what I did?" After beating up Vince, I thought Wayne would hate me, but he gave me something closer to respect. I fell in love with Wayne, and he knew it. Abi warned me to stay away. Weston begged me to have some common sense. But I was in love and couldn't see the cruelty behind Wayne's smile.

Inhale. Stop thinking about Wayne. *Exhale.* Stop thinking!

"There ain't no good reason for a kid doing what you done," Dale says. "Honest, Raleigh, sometimes I think you're just unlucky, other times I reckon you're rotten, gathering more rot like your roadkill gathers flies." He pauses, his expression sliding from anger into resignation and he shakes his head. "Get this cleaned up or God help me—" Dale bites back his words and throws me a parting glance that would strip the bark from a tree before striding back to the house. Madison stands on the porch with Nashua in her arms. I'm glad I can't see her expression from here. I'm not afraid of Dale. He wouldn't dare lay a hand on me, not only because Maddy would divorce him on the spot, but because he knows I'd break both his hands faster than he could swing them, not that he would. Dale's never been a fighter, so unlike our father, which is probably why Maddy married him.

"Let me help." Crow joins me as I start sweeping up glass. I study the broken bat. A crack that extends all the way to the handle.

"Are you hurt?" I ask.

"Not really." He rolls his shoulders. "Did you see something?" He lowers his voice, casting furtive glances at the others returning to their rooms now that the show's over.

"You getting naked with a boy called Jeremy."

"Really?" Crow's head shoots up, and he looks surprised.

"Does that shock you?" I ask a little more defensively than I should.

"Nope, just confirms what I already suspected." A faint smile slides across his face.

"What did you see?" I start washing the blood off Bear. What he already suspected? My minds chews on that until Crow's next word.

"Wayne," he says. "You had a major crush on him, and I can see why. He could've been Captain America."

It was impossible not to crush on Wayne, not to breathe more deeply when he passed me in the halls, impossible not to want him. But I can't think about Wayne. Not with Crow standing so close to me. Not with Buddy Mitchell waiting for me. Not ever.

"He's the reason you kept playing football," Crow says.

I shrug in answer, trying not to think about Wayne, although that just makes me think about him all the more—Wayne in the showers all 6'1, 220 pounds of him...naked. And he saw me, too, looked me up and down and stared straight into my eyes.

"You know, as much as this memory-share is confusing and somewhat creepy, it's kind of nice knowing someone else gets me, even if it's only for the fleeting glimpse of a memory." Crow helps me seal up the broken windows with garbage bags and duct tape.

"Let's see how you feel after you've remembered some more of my life." My gaze drifts to 206. "Thanks, by the way."

"No worries, man. You should get some ice on that." He gestures to my throbbing jaw and swollen eye. "What's with those two, anyway?"

"Apparently I irrevocably wounded Lilah when I gagged at the thought of kissing her in the fifth grade. I also sort of announced to the entire school it was because she stank of garlic. Her humiliation became a grudge, revenge-bullying, you know." I shrug it off as if I didn't spend years terrified of break time. "Eventually I fought back and ended up with Vince's teeth buried in my fists." And more, but Crow doesn't need to know the rest.

"A woman scorned, right?" Crow drags a hand through his hair and shakes his head.

"Yeah. See you tomorrow." I head up to the house and Crow ambles back to the motel. Bear hesitates before following me up to the porch. I tiptoe into the kitchen in search of a bag of frozen peas. Hushed voices drift from the lounge.

"Maddy, think of Nash. It ain't healthy for a kid."

"He's my baby brother!" Madison raises her voice only to be shh'd by Dale. I prowl closer to eavesdrop.

"He's a wreck and he's hurting this family; he's hurting

himself," Dale says. "He's unstable. My son…"

"*Our* son. And Leigh would never hurt him. Look at who he's hurt. Bullies and criminals."

"Maddy, he needs help." There it is again, that genuine concern in Dale's voice that makes me feel like shit. If he hated me and wanted me gone, it would be a lot easier, but part of me knows he actually cares.

"He saw a doctor. They took him off the meds," Maddy says.

"Maybe he needs to see someone else. I don't think taking him off was right. Maybe we need to get him in somewhere."

"He's all I have left," Madison whimpers, and regret threads through my veins.

"You have a husband and a son, darlin'." Dale soothes. "We should get Raleigh the help he needs."

"That's okay, Dale." I step into the lounge and Dale straightens up. "Just give me another coupla weeks and I'll be outta here."

"Leigh, please." Madison takes a step toward me, but Dale tugs her back down onto the sofa.

"And where're you gonna go?" he asks.

"Mars."

Dale's laughter hits me like machine gun fire. "And how in the Lord's good name are you going to afford that?"

"That's not your problem."

"You're deluding yourself," Dale says. "Get into community college, apprentice somewhere. Do something sensible and stop dreaming!"

"Like flipping burgers for the rest of my life?"

Ignoring my jibe, Dale continues, "Ain't no way you'll get into the program and when you don't, then what? You won't come crawling back here, that's for sure."

"Dale." Madison silences him with a look. "Leigh, we're just concerned about you. After tonight. Maybe you came off the meds too soon. Maybe…"

After tonight? As if I'm in the wrong. They have no idea how much I wanted to crush Lilah's skull, how hard it was not to swing that bat. I walk away. If I don't, I'm going to do something else I'll regret.

"Raleigh, wait!" Madison runs after me, but I'm out the door before she can catch me. Sometimes I envy Weston, envy that he's where he wants to be, that it was so much easier for him to switch between worlds when getting where I want to be seems increasingly impossible. Maybe I am *loco*, dreaming of Mars and helping a stranger who can't even remember his own name.

Inhale. I stare up through the neon blur of the gas station, my heart racing faster than Bear hurtling after a gopher. *Exhale.* I count the stars, giving my brain a chance to process all the weirdness of the night. *Inhale.* Mars burns against the indigo sky. *Exhale.* A few more weeks and I'll get my chance to leave this all behind. I'm so close now I can almost taste that red regolith.

Tearing my gaze from the constellations, I stride down to 206. There's a flash of movement in the window and the door opens.

"Raleigh." He greets me with that nicotine grin.

"Buddy." The word tastes like sour milk. *Think of Mars. Just think of Mars.*

"Who's your friend?" He jerks his head in the direction of 204.

"Leave him be."

"After I saved your ass, I reckon I deserve some rewardin'."

"I'm not doing it for free."

"Then I guess I'll be sayin' it was you who bust up the station and started the fight?" Buddy smirks.

"Fuck you," I bite out through clenched teeth.

"Precisely." He smirks and holds the door open. At least someone wants me. I step into his room and this time it's not about funding my dreams, it's about paying for my sins.

CROW

Bear wakes me, scratching at the door. Pooch doesn't look too bad considering he almost had his skull caved in with a baseball bat. He makes himself at home on the bed. I step into the bathroom expecting to find my shoulder black and blue. Nothing. Not a scratch. Weird. I poke the skin, waiting for my fingers to find a spot of tenderness, but they don't, only the pale beginnings of another scar, barely visible on my skin.

After a shower and spraying on a new shirt, I head outside. The sun punches me in the face and makes my head spin. Raleigh tiptoes out of 206 looking disheveled.

Whoa. That's Buddy Mitchell's room, and Raleigh's wearing the same clothes he was yesterday. Given the look of shame burning up Raleigh's face, it's not rocket science figuring out what he's been doing. Buddy Mitchell, the greasy old trucker with a beer belly and stained teeth. I shudder at the thought of his grubby fingers on Raleigh. Jesus, why did Raleigh do it? Did he want to, or did he feel like he had to? Either way, I'm struggling to understand why he'd do it, not to mention the ribbon of jealousy snaking through my chest.

"Hey." I stuff my hands into my pockets. "You okay after last night?" I try to keep the judgment out of my voice, but it's not easy.

"After which part?" Raleigh spits the words from his swollen mouth, his jaw mottled with bruising and his eye ringed purple-red. He turns to face me, fists clenched. "After Vince almost beat my head in, after Dale practically kicked me out the house, or after I let some old trucker— " He looks away.

"Why did Dale kick you out?" I'd rather focus on that than imagine Raleigh with Buddy.

"That's what you wanna know?" His words slide sideways

in his drawl. It always gets thicker when he's upset.

"It's none of my business who you sleep with, and I'm the last person to judge considering I can't remember who I've been with." I hold up my hands, waving them like white flags and wishing I believed my own words. I shouldn't judge, but I am and can't help feeling a little grossed out. I'm being an asshole, mostly because I really wanted it to be me Raleigh chose to roll around in the sheets with. "Looks like you need coffee and a cigarette."

"That sounds good." Raleigh's lips twitch and he sighs, raking his fingers through his tangled hair. "Give me twenty to get cleaned up. I'll meet you in the kitchen."

"Sure thing." I watch him walk away. I might not be able to remember my own name, but I know what I'm starting to feel for Raleigh, and it makes me want to take that baseball bat and turn Buddy Mitchell into a bloody pulp.

Half an hour later, Raleigh joins me at the diner smelling like coconut and nothing at all like greasy trucker. Maybe I can pretend it never happened.

"Does it hurt?" I graze my thumb across his injured jaw, careful not to touch him in case we get attacked by memories. The desire to kiss him is still there, although I'm a little wary now. How many others has Raleigh kissed? How many have I?

"I'm fine." He blinks and unlocks the door. "How's your shoulder?"

"Not a scratch." I lift up my sleeve to show him. "And I definitely took the hit. I thought my arm was broken."

"The bat got splintered. How're you not even bruised?" He stares at my body, his gaze shifting across the whorls and knots.

"No idea, except there's a new scar forming." I tap my shoulder and he peers closer.

"Wait, so it's not scarification?"

"Who knows?" Feels like I take two steps forward and ten steps back. I still don't even know my own name.

"That's real strange." Raleigh looks at me through ridiculously long eyelashes.

"Not the strangest thing about me." I wink as Dale stomps inside carrying an old tool case.

"We got screwdrivers, hammers, a multimeter, and just about anything else I reckon you'll be needing." Dale hands it over, completely ignoring Raleigh's presence. "There's a list of what needs fixin' inside, too."

"Thank you, sir. Anywhere you'd prefer I start?"

"Thermostat on the deep freeze has been busted for years. You get that workin' and I'd be one happy son of a gun."

"See you later?" I ask Raleigh.

"I've got some errands to run this afternoon if you wanna join me?"

"Errands?" Last time he said that I think he ended up on his knees in room 206.

"Shopping for my mom." Raleigh doesn't meet my gaze.

"Find me when you're ready to go."

Dale ushers me into the storage area and my first day on the job begins.

RALEIGH

"That boy is fine." Abi checks out Crow, who's working shirtless on the decrepit garage door. It's been broke ever since West tried teaching me to drive and accidentally put the Dodge in reverse.

"But what's with all the ink?" she asks.

"They're scars." It's taken all morning for me to feel more like myself and less like a whore. I want to believe Crow won't judge me, that knowing what I am won't change things between us, but I'm not that naive.

"He been through a wood-chipper or something?"

"Reckon it's scarification."

"You mean he deliberately got chopped up? That's nuts." She sighs and sips her Coke. Crow rolls his shoulders and we both stare. "Scars or not, he can grease my hinges any day."

"Down girl."

"What? It's not like you're making a move."

"Abigail." I roll my eyes.

"Doubt he's sticking around in Dead Rock for the tourist attractions. Haven't you seen the way he looks at you?" She flicks me with her apron before disappearing into the AC'd interior of the diner. Maybe he could've looked at me like that, but not after witnessing my walk of shame. Now he'll only look at me with disgust, or even worse: pity.

When my shift ends, I find Crow hammering the gutters over my bedroom window back into place.

"You almost done?" At least he's wearing his shirt again, which makes talking to him a bit easier.

"Damn!" He near jumps out of his skin and gouges his inner arm on a protruding nail.

"Oh hell, you okay?"

"Not sure yet." He climbs down the ladder, blood smeared

across his forearm.

"Here." I beckon him over to the hose in the roadkill garden and rinse his arm. Carefully, Crow rubs away the blood and dirt. "You might need a tetanus shot. Or not." We watch the gash on Crow's arm turn into a graze, before vanishing completely.

"Sweet mother of God, what just happened?" Crow stares at his arm like it might not be his own. "You saw that, right? It was bleeding. I felt the skin break. I mean, it hurt. And now... This is exactly what happened with my shoulder."

"And your face." I gesture to his smooth jaw where before there'd been a bloody scrape. We both keep staring at his arm.

"That's not normal." He pokes his flesh.

"You're not exactly normal."

"Yeah, but this is super whack."

"Try again." I hand over my pocketknife. Gingerly, he drags the blade across his skin.

"Do you feel it?"

"Definitely," he says. The cut seals shut and vanishes, leaving behind only a smudge of blood. Crow does it again, and again, making several gashes across his arm. They bleed and heal. It should be fear turning my stomach, fear of what this means, of what Crow might be, but my innards are doing somersaults from excitement and wonder.

"Guess that's how you survived falling out the sky." I pry my blade from his trembling fingers before he decides to do more damage and hose off his arm.

"This isn't possible." Crow's forehead is a thicket of frown lines. "Human beings don't spontaneously regenerate like that."

"No, they don't."

"What are you saying?" He glares at me.

"Nothing, just that people don't heal like that." And maybe you're an alien or have super powers. Maybe Crow is my very own Clark Kent.

"But *I* did." He stares at his arm, pumping his fist a few times. Veins rise like sandworms beneath his skin, but there's no evidence of injury. No evidence of anything to explain why Crow heals so quick.

"We already knew you were something else."

"Did we?" Dragging the ladder, he heads for the garage.

"You mean waking up naked in Texas, sharing memories with me, and all those funky scars wasn't enough of a clue?"

He slams the tool box onto the work bench and drops the ladder before turning to face me with his hands on his hips. "This isn't a joke. This is my life."

"Mine, too, considering we're sharing headspace."

"Sorry." He deflates. "This is just too much. And if I can heal like that…" He takes a step closer to me, smelling of sweat and dust and something magical, then gestures to his arm, to the perfect skin unmarked by the recent carvings. "How do you explain all the scars?"

"They're not like normal scars." I raise my hands, indicating the puffy keloid on my own wrists.

"Then what are they? Birthmarks?"

"Wish I had the answers."

"Me too." He takes a deep breath and drags his hands through his hair, leaving them at the nape of his neck.

"Feel like going for a drive?"

"Why not? It's not like I've got anywhere else to be." His frown persists as he follows me to Madison's truck. "Shopping, right?" He swings up into the cab beside Bear, who sits panting between us.

"Grocery run for my mom." Having Crow with me will be an excuse not to linger with Mama, hearing all her old stories over again, having to explain yet again that Weston is dead. She never could wrap her head around one of her children dying before she did.

"You haven't spoken about your parents much," he says.

"Not much to tell." I sigh. "Dad's fighting in the Middle East. Mom's gone nuts and lives out in the desert." I jam my phone into the port on the dashboard, and Weston's aggressive guitaring spills into the truck, his voice a melancholy balm over the angry riff.

Crow sucks in a breath and cocks his head, listening.

"What?"

"This song." A muscle flexes along his jaw dusted with stubble.

"You remember it?"

"Wasn't sure if it was a dream, but I guess it was a memory. This song's called 'Dismantling the Eons.'"

"Yup." My skin prickles.

"I remember hearing this on acoustic guitar, or I guess you did," Crow says, and every single hair on my body stands on end as that static charge between us ignites. "You and West were watching the Capricornid meteor shower. You watched the stars fall and you said it was like the universe was disintegrating, and because of the speed of light and its delay reaching Earth, it was like—"

"A dismantling of the eons."

"Exactly." Crow slumps in the seat, one hand idly stroking Bear. We let Weston's voice fill the void between us.

"Yeah, that was me and West out at the old Pontiac."

Crow stares straight ahead, his fingers digging into his knees. "Just wish we knew why or how this was happening to us."

"I'm telling you, it happened in the scrub that night."

"The bright light thing?" He tosses me a grin.

"I didn't see God, but I did feel all floaty and strange like I was getting pulled apart and put back together. The pieces didn't quite fit, but the puzzle got jammed together anyway."

"Maybe you were onto something with Lacan."

"Welcome to the desert of the Real and all?" There's no hiding my incredulity.

"Of the surreal, maybe." Leaning his head back, Crow stares at the roof of the car. "I'm still waiting to wake up from this nightmare."

"That bad, huh?" Disappointment settles in my gut like a brick, not that I was expecting Crow to be loving his time in Dead Rock.

"Well, some parts aren't bad at all."

I cast him a furtive glance over the top of Bear's head and catch him smiling at me, a sad smile, but it still heats my blood. How can he look at me with anything except contempt now that he knows what I am?

We swing by the co-op, filling the cart with long-life milk, eggs, processed meats, potatoes, and other GMO vegetables designed to survive the heat. Crow picks out some extra clothes as well and ditches the stained overalls for a pair of jeans that sit teasingly low on his hips and a T-shirt that reads "Kiss me, I'm not your cousin." It was either that, or a shirt with a confederate flag.

"Is your mom throwing a party?" Crow asks when we're waiting at the checkout. In the interest of preserving Dead Rock jobs, the co-op hasn't upgraded to automaton cashiers.

"It's a month's worth." I turn to unload the cart and lock eyes with Wayne. He's got a goatee now and some of his football muscle has melted into flab, but his eyes are just the same, piercing and beautiful.

My heart twitches like a dead roach behind my ribs and my lungs refuse to inflate. All sound fades and my vision narrows, focusing on two ice-chip points of blue. *Inhale.* I can't. He isn't supposed to be here. *Exhale.* He should be living it up in Austin where no one knows how he got his skew nose or the scar across his jaw. *Inhale.* The pain in my chest subsides as oxygen hits my lungs. *Exhale.* He's staring at me, but I can't read his expression. His gaze slides from me to Crow, and he sucks in a breath, his fingers tracing the welt of scar tissue across his jaw. A thousand things I could say march through my brain wearing hobnail boots, dying before they make it to my tongue or out my mouth. What good are words now? What's done is done, and we both have to live with the scars.

"Raleigh, hey." Crow nudges me, and I look away from Wayne as he disappears down the cereal aisle, his hair like raw sunshine exactly the way I remember it. "You okay?" He hands me a sack of potatoes.

I nod, not trusting myself to speak. My hands are shaking and if Crow wasn't here, I'd probably be bolting out the door and hightailing it home without daring to look over my shoulder. It's been more than four years and the sight of Wayne still leaves me a shivering wreck. *Inhale.* Get a fucking grip. *Exhale.* Don't let Crow see how broken you are. *Inhale.* Why not? Only a matter of time before he sees it for himself. *Exhale.*

"Was that him?" Crow asks once we're trucking out of town. "The footballer you had a crush on? He looked like the guy in your memories."

"Yeah." Swallowing hard, I turn off the asphalt and onto the meandering dirt track that snakes through the fracking lands.

"I'm guessing there's a story there. Do you want to talk about it?"

"That is precisely the last thing I wanna do." Fiddling with controls on the dash, I keep the petrochemical stench out of the climate-controlled interior and try not to think about Wayne: his hands, his breath, his body.

"God, it's barren." Crow squints out the window, apparently content not to push the Wayne issue. "Think we could swing by the crater? Doubt it'll hold the answers, but I'd like to see it for myself." And just like that, I can bury the memories and pretend to forget about Wayne, focusing on Crow instead.

"Sure." I hang a left and we barrel across the scrub, searching for smashed flowers and flattened earth. "It should be right here." I pull up and start walking.

"How can you be sure? It all looks the same." Crow raises his eyebrows.

"Someone's tried to rake it over." Despite their best efforts, the crater is still visible. Tire tracks lead away north from the impact site. Someone else knows Crow fell, and they've tried to cover it up. My palms slick with sweat and thoughts of Area 51 surface in my mind. If they know someone fell out the sky, this place should be crawling with Feds, or cordoned off from the public. But maybe that would draw too much attention. I can only hope men in suits won't be after me now, too.

"That's disconcerting." Crow shivers despite the skin-blistering heat. "It's like we've stumbled into a government conspiracy film." Dropping to his haunches, he runs a hand through the dirt.

"Feel anything?"

"Like the residual energy of an alien encounter?" He waggles his eyebrows with a smirk hanging off his lips.

"You never know. You could've been spewed out by a wormhole." I offer him my hand and an electric pulse snaps through my arm, a hundred times stronger than anything I've felt before. It knocks both of us off our feet, and the desert distorts in my peripheral vision, the scrub splintering into a series of ones and zeros.

"Do you see that?"

Crow blinks and rubs his eyes before getting to his feet and dusting off his ass. "I'm not sure what I'm seeing."

"Numbers, like code. It was the same the first night I found you."

"Code?" He stands with hands on his hips. "Next you're

going to tell me we're inside a computer game."

"It's not that far-fetched. Look—"

"You're not going to start quoting Moravec or Bostrom, are you?"

"Who are they?"

"Moravec did a lot of work in robotics and AI," Crow says, the wind blowing curls across his face. "He also believed in simulated reality, a concept Bostrom ran with."

"Sounds interesting."

"It is, but only if it isn't a way of escaping reality. We're here, Raleigh. This is real. I bleed, I hurt, and so do you. There's nothing simulated about it."

The fact that he heals makes him a lot more like one of those regenerating game characters than a human being, but I keep my mouth shut and we clamber back into the truck.

"Any luck with the stuff online?" he asks.

"Nada."

"I did some searches myself and came up empty, too." He drums his fist on the dash.

"Think it's possible that might be deliberate?"

"You mean like whoever raked over the crater is trying to erase my existence?" A black SUV passes us going in the opposite direction, and a thread of unease winds up my spine. I'm pretty sure it's the same SUV that passed me the other day, complete with tinted windows. I try to catch the plates in the rearview, but there aren't any. The unease expands into anxiety. Even Feds have license plates.

"Yeah, something like that," I say.

"Well if some government agency is on my tail, why haven't they picked me up yet? What are they waiting for?"

"Wish I knew."

Twenty miles later, we wind along the edge of a canyon, rolling up to a trailer parked between bunches of creosote. The canyon wall drops a couple of hundred feet from where we stop, the cleft in the rock like an angry god took a meat cleaver to the earth.

"It's beautiful, in a desolate, otherwordly sort of way." Crow shields his eyes with a hand as he studies the landscape. No more number smudges at the edges, just big sky and thirsty earth.

"You're hearing what you're saying, right?"

"Smart-ass." He squints at me through the glare. "Doesn't mean there are aliens sitting at PCs programming our actions."

I shrug and Bear leaps out of the cab, kicking up a plume of red dust.

"You know, there's this canyon on Mars called the Valles Marineris," I start. "It's so long, it would stretch all the way across the States if you put it on Earth. It's over four miles deep in some places. Of course, they use kilometers up there." We reach into the back for the bags, our elbows bumping.

"That's quite something," he says.

"You've just got to wonder what's down there, you know. Like, think about the weird creatures we've found in the Mariana Trench. I reckon it's just a matter of time before they find the remnants of life on Mars, and maybe they'll find the missing link to the human evolution question, like the alien chunk of DNA we originated from or—"

"Raleigh," Crow interrupts with a lopsided grin. "You have a real hard-on for Mars, huh?"

I return the grin and it feels an awful lot like flirting. Would he really flirt with me knowing who's touched me, knowing I let it happen?

"I'd do anything to join the MarsLife Corps."

"Anything." He whispers as if he understands. We trek across dying grass to the trailer, the wind knocking a whole symphony out of the chimes dangling from an open window. Bear dives into the shade under the stairs, knowing he's not welcome inside with Mama's allergies.

"Did you make these?" Crow jerks his chin at the singing bones.

I nod. They're hardly my best work.

"Sweet." He stops to admire them. "You know there aren't any bones on Mars."

"Not yet." Making wind chimes out of dead astronauts. Not a pleasant thought, and yet I kind of like the idea of my remains being turned into something beautiful instead of just rotting in the ground or getting reduced to ash. "Hey, my mom is a bit strange, like, after my brother, you know." Embarrassment warms my cheeks.

"Don't worry about it." Crow waves away my concerns and flicks indigo hair off his face.

"Mama, it's Raleigh. Open up." I knock on the door. She emerges in a tie-dye dress with her hair in three plaits. Ever since she quit civilization and moved out into the desert, she's been trying to reclaim her native heritage, or her hippie youth. She can't seem to decide which, and I don't have the heart to tell her that nothing about the way she's dressed is even remotely Comanche.

"Leigh." She squeezes me, her breath fouled by whatever herbal concoctions she calls tea. "What happened to your face?" She pulls my chin left and right, examining my jaw and eye. "This your daddy's doing?"

"No, Mama." He's been on tour for over a year already. Besides, he never hit me. West got all of that. I sneak a glance at Crow. I don't want to know what he must think of me, a messed up redneck with a *loco* mother living in a trailer in the desert.

"Did you bring me my bananas?" she asks, my injury forgotten.

"Got them here, ma'am." Crow raises the bag in his hand.

"Who's this fine-lookin' fella?" Mama extends her arms to Crow, squishing him in a hug. I give him an apologetic look, but he just smiles.

"I'm Crow."

"Crow." She whistles. "Fine name, that. Crows are clever birds, one claw in this world and one in the next."

"I think that's fairly accurate." Crow catches my eye as we trundle into the trailer. It stinks as usual, a dizzying, herbal miasma that makes my nose itch and head ache even with the breeze cutting through the windows. Mama doesn't believe in modern amenities except for her phone, which she uses to order supplies from me and read about Peyotism online.

"Tell me about yourself, Crow. How'd you meet my Raleigh?" Mama pulls out a stool for him, settling opposite at the tiny kitchen table while I pack away the groceries, cramming them into her shoebox sized pantry.

"I met him here in Dead Rock," he says.

"You don't sound like you're from Texas, son."

"No, ma'am, I guess I'm not."

"That couple weren't from 'round here neither. Guess tourism is picking up."

"What couple?" I shut the refrigerator hard enough to knock off Mama's old-fashioned magnets and a few e-cards cycling through images of Indian art.

"Owen and Tempest. Said they were from some or other outreach program. Guess someone told them about me living out in the trailer, and they thought I needed charity, or soul-saving."

"Did they drive an SUV?" The suspicion rolls over me thick as honey.

"How'd you know that?" she asks.

"Did the woman have a soldier-style haircut?"

"She sure did." Mama busies herself with tea-making.

"Raleigh, what's wrong?" Crow says.

"I've seen them. They were at the diner, and I've seen that SUV more than once, too."

"No missionaries ever eat at the Rusty Inn before?"

"Not in suits, and they sure as hell don't drive a black SUV with tinted windows and no license plates."

"Okay." He lowers his voice. "Think they might be the ones who flattened the crater?"

"Possible."

"I was fixin' to make some dinner." Mama grabs all the ingredients for a salad and Crow starts drooling. My thoughts churn while Crow chops tomatoes and Mama washes lettuce.

"So other than spreading goodwill, what did those folks want?" We settle down to eat.

"They were asking if I'd seen the light. All this hokey reborn stuff."

Seen the light. Like the bright blue light when Crow landed?

"Anything else?"

"They left a card in case I wanted to get in touch." Mama plucks a rectangular piece of plastic from the fruit basket. A phone number on a gray and black background—that's it.

"What do you think?" I show the card to Crow.

"Not a lot to go on." He crunches through a mouthful of rabbit food.

"Mama, did they say anything else, like where they're from or how they found you?"

But Mama's moment of lucidity is over, and she starts babbling about the virtues of some or other cactus and the recently legalized derivations thereof. Thankfully, she doesn't mention anything embarrassing. Not that it matters when Crow has uncensored access to my memories.

"Thanks for dinner, Mama." I kiss her cheeks and she hugs me tight, releasing me only to pull Crow in for a squeeze.

"Tell Weston I expect him next time," she says. "Tell Madison her Mama misses her."

"She misses you, too," I say into the wind before climbing

into the pickup after Bear. She waves to us until the distance turns my mother into a pixel on the horizon.

"Your mom's nice," Crow says.

"She's lost it."

"From all the herbs?"

"From all the grief."

"Losing your brother."

"And then some." I leave it at that. There's only so much I can handle Crow knowing about me in one day.

"Seeing your mom made me think, though."

"Yeah?" My stomach tightens, my whole body braced for what Crow might say next.

"I want you to remember more for me and it only seems to happen when we touch for an extended period of time, so…"

"You want to touch me?" For an extended period of time. *Inhale.* He can't really mean it. *Exhale.* Awkward silence.

"Raleigh."

"No, I get it. I bent over for Buddy Mitchell. You'd be nuts to *want* to touch that." Don't think I've ever hated myself as much as I do right now. "Despite all extra-curricular activities, I'm actually not diseased. Besides, it's not like you can catch anything from holding hands."

"You do this, don't you?"

"Do what?" I tense, the muscles rigid and cramped across my shoulders.

"Open your mouth and vomit out words without taking a moment to think."

"Am I wrong?" I glance at him.

"You're not right." He sighs. "In the interest of honesty, yes, it weirded me out knowing you'd been with Buddy Mitchell but only because—" His voice quavers and he chuckles, nervously. "Only because I think maybe I want to do more than hold your hand."

"Because you know I put out and you want some action, or…" Or what? It's stupid to even consider the possibility he might actually be attracted to me.

"Jesus, Raleigh." He pops his knuckles and shakes his head. "I'm trying to tell you I like you."

"You barely know me."

"So will you let me get to know you a little better or not?" He holds out his hand.

"Not while I'm driving."

"Then pull over," he says.

"You wanna do this right now?" I take my foot off the accelerator.

"Nefarious people in suits and a covered-up crater. It can't be coincidence. It must all be connected somehow. I need to remember. Please."

Alone on the dusty road, I pull over onto the shoulder. Settling in the seat, head back, Crow waggles his fingers at me. I get into a similar position, my fingers hovering above his. We clasp hands over Bear's back. The static charge between us builds slowly this time, and the curtains in my mind peel open.

I squint at the board as the teacher drones on about the difference between capital letters and lower case. We're supposed to be copying the alphabet. I grip the stylus in my right hand and try my best to get the squiggly shapes down on the board.

"Hey, dumb-ass," the boy next to me says. "You're meant to be doing p not q."

"I am doing p." Except the letter on my tablet doesn't look the same as the teacher's. The boy beside me keeps up the taunting, running through numerous creative variations of idiot and stupid-face.

"What's going on over here?" The teacher looms over me.

I can't be more than five years old. She seems gigantic, peering down at me over the edge of horn-rimmed glasses.

"He doesn't know his ABCs," the boy beside me says, and the entire class of kindergartners turns to look at me. I want to disappear, but I'm paralyzed in the chair with tears burning in my eyes.

"Let me see." The teacher pries the tablet from my fingers and studies my work.

"Oh dear," she says.

"Is he dumb?" the boy asks.

"No. No one is dumb, Ricky. Don't ever call someone that."

"Then what's wrong with him?" The girl behind me peers over my shoulder.

"I think it might be dyslexia." She returns the board to me.

Dyslexia! The tears fall thick and fast now and the taunts from the rest of the class continue despite the teacher's best attempts at getting them to settle down. I sprint from the classroom, chest heaving and nose full of snot to the nearest bathroom.

I have dyslexia and I'm going to die.

Crow jerks away from me, severing our connection and the snatch of memory. He opens his door and vomits into the dirt, cursing between heaves. I rummage around on the back floor and find the water bottle Maddy always keeps on hand.

"Here." I hand it to him and he takes it, careful to avoid contact before rinsing out his mouth.

"So?" I ask once he's back in the car, head resting against the seat and eyes closed.

"You first."

"I saw you in Kindergarten." I shake my head, throwing off the heartbreak of Crow as a little kid, the terror that seized him thinking he had a terminal illness. "You were convinced you were gonna die of dyslexia."

"Oh wow." He laughs, his eyes disappearing as his face scrunches up. "I think I remember that."

"Does the dyslexia still bug you?" I rifle through the glove box and pass him a stick of gum.

"Haven't noticed, to be honest. Guess I must've learned to cope with it."

"Well, obviously, academic trophies and all. Your turn." Crow starts chewing, making the cab smell like peppermint.

"I think…" He pauses mid-chew. "You were in juvie."

"I was." *Inhale.* Maybe what he saw wasn't so bad. *Exhale.* Everything that happened in juvie was bad.

"I saw them come after you, those three boys with shivs," he says. "You were so scared. Jesus. I was so scared reliving it. They cornered you in the showers. And…"

"You don't have to go on."

"I couldn't take any more of it." He shakes his head and takes another drink from the water bottle. "Did they hurt you?"

"No." I let go of the breath I've been holding. "I hurt them." And then I started letting them fuck me instead.

"I'm sorry."

"What for?" I fire up the truck and pull back onto the road.

"For what they did to you, and for getting you into this whole memory-sharing mess."

"We'll figure this out." God, I hope so.

"I don't think the memory thing we get from touching each other is going to be enough. It's too random and too…"

"Painful?"

"Intimate." Crow seems to chew on his next words as well as the gum before spitting them out. "And for the record, whatever you choose to do with your body is none of my business. It doesn't change the fact that I consider you a friend."

That's got to be one of the nicest things anyone has ever said to me. I wish I could respond, but right when I need them, words fail me and I end up nodding instead.

Friend. Does that mean there's zero potential for being more than friends? That I'm still thinking about that possibility only confirms how delusional I am.

"Should we call that number?" His fingers drum against the dash.

"Do you want to?"

"I want answers, so yeah. Maybe."

"They've gotta be Feds or some division of the government." I turn onto the interstate.

"What do they want with me?"

"A guy who can spontaneously heal with ties to the Bennett Institute and MarsLife program?" I fish the plastic rectangle from my pocket and slide it across the dashboard.

"What are you implying?"

"Just trying to connect the dots."

"The more I think I know, the less it makes any sense." He takes the card from me and rubs a thumb over the glossy plastic. "None of it makes sense."

"Ah shit." Blue and red lights draw lazy circles across the asphalt at the Rusty Inn. Dale and Madison stand in conversation with two officers.

"Are they here for you?" Crow sinks lower in his seat. "Or me?"

I swallow the granite hunk of fear in my throat and park outside the station.

"Guess we're gonna find out."

"That's him." Dale points at Bear where he trots at my heels, tail wagging. Crow hangs back, leaning against the truck. No point in him getting mixed up in my shit-storm.

"Raleigh Williams." Sergeant Daniels looks me up and down before his gaze rests on Bear. His hand slides toward his 9mm. "Call it in, Pete."

"Call what in?" Fear shreds my insides faster than a twister tearing through a trailer park. This has to be about the other night. They can't arrest me. It was self-defense.

Inhale. Please don't arrest me. *Exhale.* Anything but another arrest.

"Heard about the trouble you had with the twins." Daniels sifts saliva through his teeth. "Been talking to Mr. Buckner here, and I think we've got a pretty good picture of things." The sergeant turns to Dale for corroboration.

"They're the ones that started it." My voice hitches up an octave. An animal control truck rolls in behind the police car and my blood turns to acid, burning me inside out.

"Raleigh acted in self-defense," Crow says, joining me in my face-off with Daniels. Part of me wants to hug him for standing up for me; another wants to tell him to keep a safe distance.

"We know that, son." Daniels looks Crow up and down before he gestures to the AC officers. "But the Mulhoneys have agreed to fair compensation. We're just here for the dog."

"You're taking my dog?" The bottom falls out of me, leaving me hollow and empty.

"You can't do this," Crow says with enough vehemence for the both of us.

"We've got a warrant." Pete slaps a NeoTab into my hands, and Bear's hackles rise, a deep growling resonating from his belly.

"Raleigh, do as they say," Dale says. "Or the Mulhoneys will press charges."

"*They'll* press charges? We should be pressing charges."
I stare at the paperwork, at the scrolling lines of text and the
flashing red box waiting for my biometric signature.

"I don't want no trouble now." Dale holds up his hands
in surrender.

"But they destroyed your store and attacked Raleigh."
Once again Crow comes to my defense, directing his disbelief
at Dale.

"And this here dog near tore off Miss Mulhoney's hand,"
Daniels says. "Chewed up her leg real good, too. The hospital
issued the complaint on her behalf. Forty-four stitches she's
got. And this ain't the first time we heard about a pit roaming
off leash 'round these parts. You know that's against the law."

"What law?" I can't breathe. They've come for my dog.

"Dangerous dog law," Pete chips in. "Animal like that
oughta be chained up and behind a fence, not running wild."

"Bear was only guarding his property," Crow says.

"Who are you again, son?" Daniels narrows his eyes and
Crow clenches his jaw.

"My dog has never hurt a soul." My hands tremble, the
words demanding I hand over Bear to the authorities blur as
tears of rage burn in my eyes.

"Lilah might disagree. And we know your dog's history,"
Daniels says, and the animal control officers advance. "We
don't got no choice. Fighting dogs like that shouldn't be pets."

"You can't do this." I toss the NeoTab into the dirt and
hook my fingers in Bear's collar. He whines and presses
against my legs.

"Christ, Raleigh. You want them to take *you* instead?"
Dale throws his hands in the air. "You want us to lose this
place?" He waves at the Rusty Inn. "Because we don't got no
money for lawyers." There it is again, that genuine concern
that makes me feel bad just for breathing.

"Raleigh." Crow's hand hovers above my shoulder, his

eyes brimming with sympathy—or is that pity?

"You can't take him." Crouching, I wrap my arms around Bear. He licks my face. I can't lose him. I won't. It wasn't his fault he was born in the fighting ring.

"Come on, kid." The animal control officer gives me a sad smile, his teeth far too white against his black skin. "It's for the best."

"You're going to kill him." My heart shrivels in my chest, a rotten core. Dale was right. There's nothing good in me.

"In situations like this, it's order of the court that the dog be put down. Unless you want to appeal—"

"No, we don't," Dale cuts off the sheriff. "You do this, it's over, right? No charges, no more trouble for Raleigh?"

"Yes, sir," Daniels says.

"Then we'll comply." Dale's words are spears, pinning me to the ground. I crush Bear to my chest.

"Please. Please don't do this."

The AC officers reach for Bear with their leash poles. Maybe it's my fear, my anger making it worse, but Bear lunges, lashing out with teeth and claws like he used to when they kept him in the cage, beating on him to toughen him up. I know exactly how he felt.

"Raleigh, for Christ's sake!" Dale yells. Bear almost gets his jaws around the AC officer's wrist. He steps closer and lowers his voice, "How're you gonna get to Mars if you're up at the Creek? Think about your future, son."

Crow gives me a subtle shake of his head as if he knows what's going through my mind.

If I could, I'd take them all on. I'd pound each one of their ugly mugs into the asphalt, stomp them out of existence and let Bear lick up the scraps. There's a vast chasm below me, and I'm teetering on the precipice. Half a step closer and I'll fall, I'll plummet into a darkness so absolute there'll be no coming back, no way of ever reaching for the light, or for Mars.

"Bear, leave." My voice cracks and he stops snarling. "Do you have to take him?" I ask. "I mean, if you want him dead, can't I just do it here?"

The officers exchange worried glances with Daniels. Dale rubs his hands over his face and shakes his head.

"You sure are a piece of work, son." Daniels spits into the dirt. "But no. There's protocol and paperwork. You know how it is. Gotta be done humanely."

"Can Raleigh at least have his body?" Crow says. "Afterward, I mean." I want to thank him but I don't trust myself to speak.

"I can't. I'm done here." Dale strides back to the diner, a dozen faces glued to the glass watching the spectacle, watching me hand my best friend over for the slaughter.

"For burial?" the AC officer asks.

"Yeah," I manage to say despite everything that's threatening to choke me.

"We can do that." He gives me an apologetic nod and reaches for the leash-pole.

"Don't." With a grunt of effort, I scoop up my fifty pound dog and carry him over to the truck. It's air-conditioned and the cages are padded. Nothing like a comfortable ride to death. As I latch the cage, Bear whines, licks my fingers, and looks at me with eyes that have always forgiven me even when no one else could. He doesn't deserve this. It should be me on the way to execution, and maybe one day it will be. After the incident with Wayne, Dad reckoned I'd be on death row before I was twenty-five. In a weird way, I think he respected me for it the way he never respected West for being the good son.

"Time to go." Crow pulls me away from the truck, his touch a Taser zap before he releases my arms. Bear smiles, drool spilling down his jowls and his tail wagging at the excitement of going for a ride.

Pete holds out the NeoTab and I only just manage to press my thumb to the screen before an imaginary fist closes around my throat, shutting off my air.

"Here, Raw." Abi materializes beside me and presses a bottle of water into my hands. I can't breathe, I can't think, I can't… There's a pain ripping through my chest, a pain I never thought I'd feel again, not after Weston, not after the doctors and all their drugs.

"Shh." She rubs my back. "It's gonna be okay. Just breathe, Raw."

I force down a mouthful of water and suck in a lungful of oxygen. The red and blue lights fade and diners return to their Tex-Mex.

"It'll be okay, Raw." Abi's crying, her face streaked with mascara, her purple contact lenses threatening to pop out of her eyes. "It'll be okay."

"No, it won't." I jerk away from her and start running.

CROW

"Is this your doing?" A voice floats out of the ether as I pull Raleigh away from the van.

"Partly. I initiated the attack on the station." The voice, familiar now, responds. **"The agents are mine, too."**

"Expected reaction?"

A crackle of static.

"Good, continue." The voices fade, carried away by the breeze and my insides turn to rocks. I cast about the lot, searching for the source of the disembodied voices, searching for something to explain what the hell is going on. Cops and Raleigh's family and a bunch of onlookers, but no one's close enough to have whispered all that in my ear. Whoever said it was responsible for Vince and Lilah, so they're responsible for Bear getting taken, too.

Raleigh takes off, and I'm left staring after him, feeling utterly helpless.

"Well don't just stand there!" Abigail glares at me. "Go after him."

My feet start moving before my brain has time to process exactly what I'm doing.

"Raleigh!"

He ignores me and plows through the scrub. Damn, the guy's fast. Hardly a surprise considering the way he used to play ball. I, on the other hand, am grossly unfit and slow to a jog to keep from having a heart attack. At least I'm able to follow the dust cloud left in Raleigh's wake. Soaked in sweat and caked in dirt, I eventually catch up with him. He's on his knees beside a dilapidated Pontiac squatting forgotten and disintegrating in the sand. I know this place. It's where he and West watched the meteor shower, where they used to hang out to avoid their father.

"Raleigh?"

"West and I used to come out here to stargaze," he says, head tilted to the darkening sky. "We kept Bear here those first few nights. My dad beat the crap outta West when he found out we were treating a fighting dog like a pet."

My heart breaks for him, a slow motion shatter as he stares with tear-stained eyes at the wrecked car. He staggers to his feet and drives his fist into the pitted steel of the hood.

"Raleigh, don't." I rush to his side.

He smacks alternating fists into the hood, not pausing even when his knuckles start bleeding.

"That's enough." I grab his arm and spin him around to face me.

"It hurts." He whimpers like a kicked puppy. "It hurts so much."

"I know." I wrap my arms around him, the prickly beginnings of a borrowed memory starting in my fingers and surging up my arms until they obliterate my mind, replacing my thoughts with Raleigh's.

There's an inch of snow on the ground when Wayne punches me in the gut and shoves me face-first into the earth. He asked me to meet him out here. I thought maybe he liked me and didn't want anyone to know, that we'd end up making out under the mesquites, but if he does like me, he sure has an odd way of showing it.

Blood and snow fill my mouth; his chili breath huffs against my ear. Somewhere to my left, Lilah has her phone at the ready. Wayne shoves his hands down my pants, peeling away my clothes and my pride. How many times did I imagine this kind of intimacy with another boy? How many times was that imaginary lover Wayne? But not like this. I could fight back, but I'm paralyzed, frozen in fear like a bait-dog about to get ripped apart. Lilah laughs as I squirm against the weight on my back, struggling to reclaim the tattered shreds of my dignity.

"Do you like that, squaw?" Wayne's lips are rough against my ear. "Is this what you wanted?"

The memory fades and Raleigh slumps against the wheel arch, resting his ruined hands on his knees. Holy shit, they assaulted him. Not some hazing ritual gone wrong, but a deliberate and planned attack. But why? Revenge for Raleigh beating up Vince? At least that's what Raleigh thinks, but I'm not convinced.

Lilah took photos of what Wayne did. Video, too. They laughed as they destroyed him. No wonder Raleigh reacted the way he did bumping into Wayne at the store. Fury ignites in my belly, pulsing heat along every capillary. They got away with it. Raleigh got eight months in juvie and a lifetime of heartache; all Wayne got was a skew nose. Hardly justice. And yet, the way he looked at Raleigh in the store makes me think the guy might be living with his own set of demons, not that that remotely vindicates him of what he did.

I'm on a roller-coaster, plowing through various emotions from outrage to devastation, from wanting vengeance to wanting to forget. They're Raleigh's emotions, sloughing away as I shake off the spiderweb strands of the memory, but the ineluctable truth remains: Raleigh was raped and hasn't told a soul. It's a weight that settles inside me—and I don't know what to do with it. I have no words of comfort to offer Raleigh, and I know from being inside his head that the last thing he wants is pity.

Once my pulse returns to normal and the trauma of reliving Raleigh's experience subsides, I join him beside the car.

"Anything deadly out here?" I ask. "Snakes, scorpions?" Warily, I scan the ground before crouching next to him.

"Just me." He meets my gaze. I don't know how to handle this. I have no idea what I'm supposed to say. Gently, I lift a shaking hand off his knee and rub away a smear of blood. An electric tingle sends a Mexican wave through my body hair and a new memory crests over me: a psychologist's waiting room, watching the minutes tick by, a prescription, pills popped, emotions numbed, and the knowledge that Raleigh thinks he's broken, that he's worthless and deserved what he got—Wayne's retribution for Raleigh knocking out his cousin's teeth.

The memory evaporates and I'm left holding Raleigh's hand. His gaze sends shock waves down my spine, his eyes bistre marbles. I brush a kiss across his knuckles.

"What—?" His voice catches in his throat, and I turn his hand over to kiss the scars on his wrist. Fresh tears gather in his eyes as I cup his face. Kneeling between his legs, I lean forward and kiss his lips. An electric jolt sends a sizzling rush along every nerve.

"Stop." The word is a whisper, and I instantly back off.

"I can't… I can't do this." He looks at me with longing in his eyes. Every nerve screams at me, the static tingle becoming more painful the longer our physical contact continues, but I don't care. I won't let go, not now.

"Why not?"

"How can you even think of kissing me when you know where my mouth's been?" he asks, reminding me of things I'd rather not think about. "Or is it because you know I'm a whore?" His words are sharp as sabers.

"That's not it at all."

"Then why?"

"I can't explain it, but…" I take a deep breath, tasting the heat and the desert. "I know how I feel every time I look at you."

"And how do you feel?"

"I've seen inside your life. You've seen mine, more of mine than I even have." I feel naked in front of him, exposed and vulnerable, and I know he must be feeling something similar. "Something special, something *cosmic*, is happening between us. Hell, isn't it enough that I want to kiss you?" And hold him and make everything better.

"You must've hit your head real hard." His tone loses its flinty edge.

"I've seen your memories, Raleigh. You don't scare me." Yes he does, but not in the way he might think he does.

"I'm the guy who fucks for money, who spent eight months in juvie, and the last three years on anti-psychotics after nearly killing a kid with his bare hands." His words flow thick and fast. "You still wanna touch me?"

"Yes." And I do, because Raleigh didn't deserve what they did to him, and he's worth a hell of a lot more than whatever his johns are paying. "I've seen you in those moments. I've *been* you. I know how much you wish your life could be different, how you'd do anything to make your dream a reality."

"What exactly did you see?" he asks, the wind whipping hair across his face.

"Enough. And I want to know more." Desperately, I do, because somehow it's in getting to know Raleigh that I get to know myself.

"You're *loco*."

"Well." A smile quirks up my lips. "I'm not sure I care." This time when I kiss him, he doesn't pull away. I open my mouth to his and his tongue darts between my teeth, his fingers knotting in my hair. He pulls me to my feet and I let him take control. He needs this, needs to know he's the one calling the shots.

Raleigh shoves me against the hood, leaning into me as he trails kisses along my jaw to bite my ear, my palms pressed to the muscular contours of his back. That feels so damn good. He kisses me harder, his hands under my shirt. I run my fingers up and down his body. God, he's ripped: abs, lats, biceps, and that awesome V disappearing into his pants, but I try not to get swept up in the moment, letting him take the lead.

Another memory hijacks my thoughts, and I tumble into it.

The splintering of a guitar, my father's voice raised in whisky-laced anger. He calls Weston a good-for-nothing waste of space, saying he'll never amount to nothing. The meaty smack of fists against flesh, and Mama yelling at them to stop.

I cower in the shadows of my bone garden, my arms wrapped around Bear. Weston runs out of the house, nose bleeding and tears streaming down his face. I run after him as he heads for the truck. He gets in and sobs behind the wheel. I tap on the window and he lowers it, not even trying to hide his tears, not caring about the blood and snot pouring off his face.

"I can't keep living like this, Leigh. I can't." His voice hitches, and he shakes his head, wiping at the mess on his face with his T-shirt.

"I know."

"I've gotta get out of here. I think he might actually kill me this time." He puts the keys in the ignition and the truck grumbles. My father staggers from the house, shaking off Mama's hands.

"Weston Indiana Williams! You get your sorry ass back here!" Dad yells.

"Get to Mars, Leigh. Whatever you do, promise me you'll get to Mars. Remember what I said about my ashes?"

"I promise." But I don't want to think about my brother dying.

"Good. You better keep your promise, Leigh. I'm counting on you." He throws the truck into reverse and pulls away as Dad rushes into the parking lot. I watch my brother drive away, hear my dad yelling curses and my mom's frantic cries, and I know that I'll never see my brother again. Something in me just knows.

I'm falling, tumbling into darkness and the earth rushes up to meet me. There's an explosion of blue and I hit the ground.

Raleigh kisses me, bites my bottom lip, flicks his tongue against my teeth, and I pull him closer. I have no idea what this is, but I want it. I want him, oh God, I want him so much my bones ache.

Raleigh lifts me onto the hood and the steel of the car sears the backs of my legs, burning through my jeans. I wrap my knees around his hips and his hand rests on my belt buckle. He hesitates and I fold my fingers over his, lifting them off my crotch. Breaking away, he looks at me, a myriad of emotions splayed across his face.

"Hey, slow down," I say.

"I thought you wanted me?" He frowns.

"I do, but not like this. You're not that boy in the snow." And although I'm not sure what kind of guy I am, I'm not going to let Raleigh screw me over the rusted bonnet of this jalopy. I trace the injuries on his face and kiss his sun-cracked lips. He tastes of dust and sunshine.

"You saw that?" he asks, and I answer him with a kiss. He kisses me back, gently this time although his hands tighten their grip on my legs, nails digging into denim. On second thought, maybe I wouldn't mind letting him have me right here, right now, except there's a tiny voice in the back of my mind reminding me I don't have a condom and that that's probably a good idea, all things considered.

"If you're worried about STDs, I've always been super careful." He seems to read my mind. "MarsLife wouldn't take me if I had anything. I get tested all the time."

"It's not that." Although I'm relieved to hear it. "I just don't think we're in any rush."

"I'm so afraid," he whispers, and I kiss his neck. "So afraid to let go in case you disappear like every other good thing in my life."

"I'm not going anywhere." It's not a promise I should make, not even one I'm sure I *can* make, but right now there's nowhere I'd rather be. Raleigh leans into me, his body hot and hard, his fingers in my hair, and his mouth crushing mine.

RALEIGH

I'm so nervous I can taste the rising bile at the back of my tongue. Swallowing it down, I step into the living room.

"Mom, Dad, do you have a minute?"

"Sure, hon. What's up?" Mom mutes the TV and Dad closes his laptop.

"Um." I run a trembling hand through my hair and perch on the edge of the sofa so I'm facing my parents. "There's something I need to tell you."

Mom and Dad share a worried look and shift closer to each other.

"Is this about Sarah?" Mom asks. Sarah, who's been my best friend forever and my girlfriend for the last three months. It took me two weeks to figure out why our relationship could never work, another two to confide in her, and the rest of the time we've been together I've been building up the courage to confront my parents.

"Yes."

"Is she pregnant?" Mom asks, her face drawn as she grabs my dad's hand.

"Mom! No." God, no. Firstly, the thought of being a father at fourteen is appalling and secondly, well that's why I'm here. Mom looks relieved, but Dad sits up and leans forward.

"What is it, son?"

There's no easy way to say this other than to come right out with it.

"I'm gay."

Mom and Dad both blink. Once, twice, and then they laugh. I'm not sure how to feel about that. They bow their heads together and have a good ol' chuckle at my expense.

"Something funny?" I ask.

"No. It's just, well." Dad clears his throat. "Well, your

mother and I have always suspected as much."

"We're just relieved, honey."

"Relieved?" This was not the reaction I had anticipated. Not that I expected them to have an apoplexy, being the liberal types they are, but I didn't expect laughter and smiles.

"You looked like someone had died. I thought you were going to tell us you'd got a girl pregnant or set fire to the school," Dad says.

"So you're not mad?"

"Mad?" Mom frowns. "Good Lord, kiddo. We love you and we want you to be happy. Gay, straight, or anything in between."

"But the rules still apply," Dad lays down the law. "No boys in your bedroom with the door closed and just because pregnancy is out of the equation doesn't mean you don't have to use a condom."

Urgh, not a conversation I ever want to have again. Mom pulls me into a hug, and Dad claps me on the back before asking, "Have you finished your homework?"

I wanted something that wasn't Dead Rock, that wasn't blood and nightmares and desert dirt and here he is, lying in my arms. I don't even care it's so hot it feels like I'm getting boiled alive or that we're sweating out an ocean lying wrapped up like this. For a moment, he's mine and that's all that matters. Later we can worry about who and what he is and what getting tangled up in each other might mean for my getting to Mars.

I'm not that boy in the snow— I want to believe it, but I'm not sure I can.

Envy ties green knots around my heart. Crow had a good life. If only my father had ever looked at me the way Crow's dad looked at him, with a mixture of chest-busting pride and unconditional love. Maybe Dad did once. There was a glimmer of something like grudging respect on his face the day they slapped me in cuffs, but his love certainly wasn't unconditional.

"Morning." Crow sits up with a groan.

"Hey." I rub the sleep from my eyes and stretch my protesting limbs, cramped from the night spent in the back of the Pontiac.

"Did you know Phobos is actually getting closer and closer to Mars," he says.

"I did indeed." Wincing, I manage to straighten my fingers, cracking open scabs across the knuckles. It's an unwelcome reminder that yesterday was real, that it wasn't a nightmare. Bear is really gone.

"Scientists predict that one day it'll collide with the planet." Crow slides out of the car and pees into a huddle of dying grass.

"Better not happen while I'm up there."

Crow grins over a patterned shoulder. I can't stop staring at his naked back, at the repeated whorl cut into his flesh. Part of me wishes he had undressed me last night. I would've let him do whatever he wanted. Except, Crow doesn't see me as a whore, and I don't want to be the one to change his mind. The scars on his back stand out in perfect contrast to his pale skin, lilac against ivory.

"Hey, come here. I wanna see something."

"What is it?" Crow sits and I trace the dingbat symbols down his spine, breaking off contact before we get mind-jacked.

"There's definitely a new one." I outline a spiral knot clearly visible on a previously unmarked patch of shoulder. It's exactly where he caught the end of Vince's baseball bat. "This wasn't here when I took the photos." Its edges aren't as distinct as the others.

"So they can't be birthmarks, either, then." He shudders as I run my finger across the scar tissue. No spongy mound of keloid, just silky skin even smoother where the patterns lie.

"What are we thinking now, alien parasite, extra-terrestrial herpes?" he asks with a grin.

"If only herpes looked half this good." My gaze moves up his spine to his neck, and my hand moves inadvertently to the same spot on my own. "What about tech? Maybe you've got some kind of implants or cybernetics?"

"What makes you think that?"

"No idea." Totally came out of left field, and yet I can't shake the feeling that I might be right.

"Ah, crap. These are new, too." Twisting, Crow shows me the inside of his forearm. Sure enough, new spirals cut through his skin. "Man, why now? You think it's because of us?"

I raise an eyebrow at that. "Think it's a coincidence the new marks have appeared where you got hurt?"

"Probably not." Crow studies his arm, the symbols lying exactly where he cut himself with my pocketknife.

"Wanna see a doctor?"

"I feel fine, and they're not bugging me." He pulls on his shirt.

"Your choice, but if I start sprouting weird symbols, we're heading to the ER. Deal?"

"You think I'm contagious?" His face pales, turning the band of freckles across his face into dark constellations.

"Let's hope not." Maybe I should be more concerned, scared even, but I'm not. I'm not sure I'd really care if I did start sporting strange symbols. Not today at least. Not when caring about this means caring about everything else and getting crushed by all the things I no longer have. What about the things I do have? Weston's dead and Bear will be soon, but I've got Crow and, even if he disappears, I'll still have Mars. I'll always have Mars and my dream.

"I saw more stuff," I say, needing to break the awkward silence.

"Am I going to like it?" Crow pops his shoulders.

"You came out to your parents." I pry myself from the collapsed seats.

"Did they freak out?" Cocking his head to the side, he frowns.

"Nope. They were just relieved you hadn't burned down the school."

"Cool, I guess." He scratches at the stubble dusting his jaw.

"Have you seen any more of my memories?" I ask with trepidation.

"I saw the night Weston died. It's not your fault, Raleigh."

"Part of it is." I avoid eye contact.

"You didn't make the choice for him."

"No, but I didn't make his life any easier. I was a coward." The floodgates open and out pours my confession. "I liked being my dad's favorite. I was afraid of standing up for West because I didn't want my dad to hit me, or worse, to stop loving me."

"What was his problem with Weston anyway?"

"West wanted to be a musician. He refused to play ball, hated the military, and wasn't shy about airing his views on politics."

"So your being gay wasn't a problem?"

"My father didn't give a shit so long as I played football. Also, I beat up kids and got sent to juvie so I proved I was tough. I think he was sort of proud of me in a warped way."

"That's really messed up." He jams his hands into his pockets.

"We should head back. Stuff to fix, robots to babysit." Which means going back to the Rusty Inn, seeing Bear's empty chair on the porch and the half-chewed boot. The pain is an eagle claw reaching from the shadows. The talons sink into my flesh and unravel the threads holding me together. One night wrapped around Crow isn't going to change my reality, and it's not like the world stops spinning for a broken heart.

"Raleigh, thank you. For helping me even with everything else going on in your life."

"You said it, we share a cosmic connection." And Crow's a welcome distraction. Even so, my mind's plotting a million different ways to get back at Vince and Lilah and make them pay for what's happening to Bear, only—MarsLife. I've got to stay focused on my goal. Keep my eye on target as Coach always said, and that target burns 225 million kilometers away.

"I'm just glad we've got each other." Crow kicks his toe through the dust.

"Only until you figure out who you are and realize you oughta be a hundred thousand miles away from this shit hole." And a million miles from me.

"You know…" he says, and we start our trek through the scrub. "There's nothing stopping you from coming with me."

"Are you serious?" This guy's nuttier than a port-o-potty at a peanut festival.

"What's keeping you here when there's a whole world out there?"

"I wanna go to Mars."

"Have you traveled at all?" His question sounds more like an accusation.

"Never been outside Texas."

"Seriously?" Crow catches my hand and tugs me to a stop, letting go when the charge crackles between us. "You've never been outside the state and you want to leave the planet?"

"I wanna get as far away as I can from Dead Rock."

"What about China or Australia?"

"I'd rather go to Mars."

Crow bites his bottom lip, and all I want to do is kiss him, to forget about everything else except the taste of his lips and the feel of his skin.

"Is it because of what your brother said?" he asks.

"That, mostly."

"I get it, Raleigh, I do. But did you ever think there might be more to life on Earth? Hell, skiing in the Alps or diving in the Great Barrier Reef."

"Speaking from experience?"

"Maybe. I don't know." He tugs a hand through his hair. "There's so much worth experiencing on Earth." I must be imagining the crease of hurt around his eyes and the knot in my gut. Going to Mars means leaving Crow behind. For the first time, there's something that might be worth staying for: not Australia or skiing in the Alps, but a guy who gets me.

"I made a promise to West and I intend to keep it." Ashes and a dream. Mars, my final destination. It would be ten kinds of crazy to change my plans for a shot at something more with Crow, and yet I can't shake the feeling that maybe I'd want to try if I hadn't given West my word.

"Even if you've got more to live for right here on Earth," he says, as if sneaking a peek at a few of my memories suddenly makes him an expert.

What have I got? Not a whole heck of a lot, that's for sure, except the memories of a total stranger, a total stranger whose kisses set me on fire. Sooner than I'd like, Crow'll figure out who he is and realize he never should've looked at me sideways. But it's nice having him look at me like a person and not just a piece of ass, like I'm more than just a rap sheet and a list of fuck-ups. Might as well enjoy what I've got while I've got it even if it means dying inside all over again the day he says goodbye.

CROW

The kitchen smells like chamomile and aniseed, the pungent steam wafting from a pair of mugs set in front of Madison and Abi. What I wouldn't give for a cup of decent coffee, Ethiopian blend, black and bitter.

Madison jumps up, knocking over her mug and ignoring the spillage. She draws Raleigh into a hug and Abi starts mopping up.

"Hey, what's up?" He pulls away to suck in a breath.

"You had me worried. When you didn't come home last night, I thought…" Her bottom lip quivers and tears clot her eyelashes. I feel awkward standing here, witnessing this outpouring of emotion. "I knew you were devastated and I just, I thought maybe, after West…" Her gaze flicks over to me then back to Raleigh. Did she tell him she tried to pay me to leave? I hope not. And I'm not going to tell him, either. She's only trying to protect him and maybe with good reason.

"I'll never do that." He hugs her again. She seems so small in his arms, frail even, but then Raleigh's arms are rather impressive. "I won't ever do what he did."

She nods.

"I'm sorry, Maddy. I didn't think," Raleigh says.

"No, you didn't." Madison swats away tears and turns her attention on me. "And… well, color me surprised," she says. "You're still here?" There's an edge to her voice letting me know unequivocally that she's not impressed by my presence.

"Those car troubles do seem to be taking a while," Abi adds with a knowing glint in her eyes.

Madison frowns and folds her arms. "Car troubles?"

"Yeah, Crow's broken-down rental, remember? The reason he got stranded in Dead Rock," Raleigh lies for me.

"Uh-huh." Madison raises an eyebrow. "Are you even old enough to sign the paperwork?"

"That's part of the problem." A nervous chuckle escapes my lips. I don't even know how old I am. If I worked at Bennett, I must at least be out of high school and I don't look older than twenty-five. "I just wanted to thank you for what you did for me and for letting me work here. I appreciate it more than you know."

"How does Mads know Crow?" Abi sets a fresh pot of water boiling.

"The first night in town I had a bit of a run-in with some local thugs and Madison was kind enough to patch me up." Madison and I share a lingering gaze.

"You're looking much better than last time." She studies my face, then my arms, and I wish I had my overalls so I could hide the scars.

"Thanks to your expertise, ma'am."

"Ma'am?" She tuts as a little boy toddles into the kitchen and tugs on the hem of Raleigh's shirt.

"How you doing today, tiger?" Raleigh scoops the kid into his arms.

"Where's Bear?" he asks in his mother's drawl.

Raleigh settles the kid into his safety seat, and I can see him struggling to spit out the words.

"He's with Uncle West, Nash," Madison says, and Raleigh swallows hard.

"In the happy humming grounds?" Nash asks with three-year-old innocence.

"Exactly. Gone to serenade the gophers." Abi reaches for Raleigh's hand. "Holy heck, Raw. What happened to your fingers?" Her gaze flicks to my face and back to his hands.

"Raleigh had a disagreement with the Pontiac," I say, and Abi relaxes.

"Is there anything left of it?" Madison *tsks* and brings out the first aid kit. Abi sets about making tea, and I settle in the chair next to Raleigh.

"Something for the swelling," Madison says to Abi.

"Just don't give me the one that smells like cat pee," Raleigh says.

"You'll drink what you get." Madison swabs antiseptic over his shredded hands. "You're lucky you didn't break any bones." She pokes and prods his knuckles, squirting ointment onto the scabs.

"I said I was sorry, Maddy, go easy." He winces.

"Don't do it again." She glares at him. "No matter what happens." Her gaze flicks past Raleigh to me as if in silent warning. "You hear me? We're family. You got it?"

"Got it." Raleigh nods.

Despite all the crap he's been through, I know Raleigh's never contemplated suicide, at least not in any of the memories I've seen. I'm not sure I could be that strong having endured what he has and still want so desperately to live, holding on to his dream. Indomitable. If I had to choose one word to describe Raleigh, that would be it. And there I go trying to tell him how good life on Earth can be for entirely selfish reasons.

Having forced down the vile contents of our tea cups and managing to avoid further interrogation from Madison, Raleigh and I stroll down to the diner.

"You shouldn't have to lie for me," I say.

"My sister won't handle the truth, or worse, she'll think I've lost it again and call my shrink."

"Did the meds actually help?"

Raleigh pauses at the bone garden and checks on his corpses. "I think they helped Maddy and Dale more than they helped me. I was easier to get along with when I was stoned."

"Because the drugs made you numb."

"You felt that?"

"I think so." I run a hand through my hair and coax out the tangles.

"It was less like not feeling and more like not caring that I felt anything. Kinda stopped my ability to react to stuff." He shrugs, his gaze lingering on the chewed-up boot.

"Do you ever miss being in that state?"

Raleigh looks at me with sad eyes. "Sometimes. But maybe it's better being able to care."

"Even when it hurts?"

"Gotta take the good with the bad, right?" He gathers up his hair and twists it into a ponytail. "If I'd been medicated, I wouldn't have felt like I did when they came for Bear. I also wouldn't have felt much of anything when you kissed me."

"So my kisses were worth it then?" If only I could kiss away all his pain.

"Were mine?" He squints up at me.

"And then some." Which only makes this suck that much harder, knowing he can't wait to get away from Dead Rock, or me.

With a smile, Raleigh goes about his work, and I head out to the laundry room. Apparently, Rosie the washer-bot has been acting up and could do with a few circuit tweaks. Halfway there, the voices assault me, louder than before as if I've got a boombox right inside my head.

"So far so good. Trials one through five are a pass." That familiar voice again.

"But not conclusive."

"Are these ever truly conclusive?"

"Conclusive enough. How long has he been under?"

"Four cycles."

"Step it up. We max out at seven."

"Hello?" I say out loud to no one. "Can you hear me?"

"Crap, there's interference."

"You can hear me!" My pulse kicks up six gears. "Who are you? What the hell is going on? I want to know who you th—"

tech1@cer-ro:~$ reboot

Raleigh

"I know it's a long shot, but do you think I could borrow your phone and call that number we got from your mom?" Crow asks while he helps me clear up the kitchen at the end of my shift. He can't stop fidgeting, his whole body twitchy and on edge.

"I kinda forgot about that." I hand over my phone. Bear getting carted away completely derailed me. I've got to get a grip else it'll be me next behind bars.

"Thanks." He slips the card out of his pocket and studies it, hesitating.

"I'll be up at the house when you're done."

He nods, and I give him some space. Abi's on the porch, sitting in Bear's chair and sucking on a cigarette.

"Can't stay away even on your off days, huh?" I join her, perched on the rickety steps at her feet.

"You remember when Bear first met me?" She offers me the cigarette. Sweet and sticky and definitely not tobacco.

"He peed in your lap."

"And Weston gave me his shirt." She gazes down at me. "You gonna smoke it or just look at it?"

"The tests are too close, but thanks." Considering drug screening is part of the MarsLife physical, the temporary high isn't worth the risk of not passing.

Wordlessly, she takes a deep drag on the joint, smoke curling out of her nose like dragon's breath.

"West had bruises." Her voice cracks. "I knew your dad was fond of the belt. Heck, my dad tanned Ford's backside more than once, but I never knew how bad it was." She joins me on the stairs, our shoulders touching. No static spark, no prickling sensation. Just Abi. She leans against me and I wrap my arm around her shoulders. "I was so mad at your father. I was mad at Weston, too, for letting it happen."

"What was he supposed to do? Fighting back would only have made it worse." And that wasn't who West was. Sometimes I think that's all my dad actually wanted, for West to finally throw a punch of his own and prove he had a spine. Dad didn't understand that being a pacifist didn't mean West was a coward. My brother was the brave one. It's easier to do the punching than take the beating.

"You think if we'd done something, if we'd told someone, things would be different?" she asks.

"Like who, Abi?" I try not to inhale the sweet tang of secondhand marijuana smoke. "My dad's military. The sheriff would've thought West deserved it."

"I just wish I'd done something. Anything. Maybe then…" She takes a steadying breath, finishing the blunt. "Maybe things wouldn't be the way they are."

"It's not your fault."

"Not only mine." She shrugs away from me. "We're all to blame. Your mama, Madison, me, you." Her words are knives and they're going to leave scars. And this time, I don't have the luxury of chemical oblivion to take away the sting of the truth. Despite what I said to Crow, sometimes I do miss floating in an un-feeling haze.

"We all could've done something," she continues. "But we didn't, and now he's dead, and so is Bear, and we could've done something about that, too."

"The sheriff has it in for me. Nothing would've changed it." I don't want to think about where my dog is right now, whether he's waiting on death row or has already been zipped up in a body bag. Dale said Daniels would call once it was all sorted. "All sorted" as if murdering my best friend is something to tick off a to-do list. My fists clench, pulling open scabs.

"Bullshit, Raw. You could've kept Bear leashed." Her

voice rises in pitch and volume. "You could've ignored Vince. You could've left Dead Rock after high school and taken Bear with you. Why'd you stay?" Abi turns on me, her eyes burning.

"Why did *you*? You and your three-point-eight. You could've gone to a real school, gone anywhere, but you didn't. You're stuck doing community college and waiting tables."

"I couldn't leave." She gnaws on a long nail. "I loved him." Her voice breaks and so does my heart. "You know what I wished when I found out West was gone? I wished I hadn't held out on him, hadn't wanted to save up my virginity until I was sure. I wished I'd slept with him and that I was pregnant, because then I'd always have a piece of him with me."

"You were just a kid."

"Well I'm not anymore and what the hell am I doing with my life? I'm still hung up on my dead high school sweetheart. I thought maybe if I stuck around, that if I couldn't have West, then maybe I could have you and I'd still get to keep a piece of him close to me."

"Abi."

"I know." She smiles through a film of tears and takes my hand. "And I love you Raw, but I'll never love you like I loved West, not when you can't love me back." Using my hand, she clambers to her feet and dusts off her shorts. "I'm leaving Dead Rock."

"What? When?" My heart wallops against my ribs, panic closing a choke hold around my throat. Abi is my anchor, but I guess I've been her ball and chain.

"I should've done it years ago. I've got a cousin in California. I need a fresh start."

"And you decided this right now?"

"I've been thinking about it for ages. This whole thing with the Mulhoneys and Bear... Now seems like the right time."

"To up and leave, just like that?" Rage burns through my veins. White-hot anger at Abi for being free to leave, for choosing to abandon me.

"Not just like that. Heck, Raw. You don't get to guilt me into staying when you're planning on being the next Deshaun Brown and hightailing it off-world."

I have no right, but it's easier being the one doing the leaving, and I thought it would be me giving the middle finger to this town.

"Why now?" My voice comes out all shaky.

"I need a change. I need my life to start. Feels like I've been churning my wheels in mud since high school waiting for my dead boyfriend to come back to life or something." She wipes away a stray tear. "You should come visit me. Finally see the ocean, you know."

"Yeah, maybe." Not that I could afford a trip out to California and MarsLife tuition.

"Well, see you tomorrow, anyhow. I'm not leaving until the weekend."

"This weekend?" Too soon. Way too soon.

"My cousin's got me a job in Sacramento. I start next Monday."

I know she's waiting for me to say something, to give her encouragement or show my support, but I can't. The words stick in my throat, strangling me. I'm losing everyone I love.

"Okay, Raw. See you." She ambles down to the parking lot. If I close my eyes, I won't have to watch her walk away like I watched Dad head off to war, like I watched Madison walk down the aisle, and Mama head off into the desert, like I watched Weston drive away and knew I'd never see him again, as clear as I know I'll probably never get to Mars, only this time I'm not going to let the knowing stop me from the trying—the way I should've tried to stop Weston from ending his life.

"Raleigh!" Abi screams as Crow staggers toward her. I leap down the stairs and catch him before he falls. He's got blood pouring out of his ears. Except the stuff isn't red, it's the color of anti-freeze. He convulses with his head in my lap.

"What happened?"I try to pin his flailing limbs.

"He came at me, all zombie-like, asking me to help him." Abi picks up my phone and the business card where Crow dropped them. "What's on his head? Sweet Jesus, that's coming out his ears."

"We've gotta get him to the hospital. Where's Madison?"

"Down at the station. You want me to get her?"

"No, leave her out of it. Can you get your pickup?"

"Two seconds." Abi bolts for the parking lot. Several agonizing moments later, she hurtles up the drive.

"Is he epileptic?" she asks once we get Crow into the cab.

"Don't know. Hey, Crow. Can you hear me?" Patting his face elicits no response.

"Mercy General?" Abi swings in behind the wheel and jams her phone into the dash.

"Yeah, and step on it. Speeding ticket's on me."

Abi floors the accelerator and guns for the interstate. I wrap my arm around Crow, resting his head on my chest. Gunk seeps out of his ears and soaks my T-shirt.

Please don't die, please don't die. The words loop on repeat in my mind. This time it's not for fear of what the cops might do to me if Crow dies in my arms, but the fear of losing him. There's no electric charge, just a sinking feeling as I drift out of reality and into something else.

I try to move, but I'm immobilized.

A woman leans over me and shines a light into my eyes.

"Can you hear me?"

I nod.

"Can you see me?"

I squint against the blinding light and nod again.

"How is he?" a man asks.

"Still coming around."

"How're you feeling, Brennan?" the woman asks.

"Thirsty." Brennan? My name, no Crow's name…

She holds a straw to my lips and I suck down mouthful after mouthful of cold water.

"Did it go as planned?" The man steps into my narrow field of vision.

"For the most part," she says.

"I can't move." My voice is rough.

"The anesthetic is still wearing off." The man pats my arm and adjusts a bandage on my head.

"What happened?"

"Get some rest," the woman says. "We'll come and check on you in a bit."

Their footsteps recede and I try to relax. I'm in a hospital. I had some kind of surgical procedure. I don't know where I am or why, but at least I'm still breathing.

No, I'm falling, floating until my feet hit solid ground. I'm standing in the crater clutching a Crow's feather. This isn't a memory. This is something else.

Squeezing my fist, the razor edges of the pinion cut into my palm. Blood drips between my fingers and I'm transported to my roadkill garden, to Bear's fresh-cut grave marked with a simple cross and his collar like a halo. The ground cracks beneath my feet, and a gnarled stem of what must be mesquite spirals out of the earth, showering me with dirt. The darkness thickens. Gaunt trees erupt from the soil, bark hanging off smooth stems in ragged strips. The trees knit above my head, their branches laced together. I wipe wetness from my face. It's not dirt; it's blood, ripe with the stench of rot.

The trees are bleeding, the tattered bark not bark at all but the remains of fur and scraps of muscle. Nausea roils in my belly. The fur is black and white. The trunks twist and creak. I run my fingers over the nearest tree. They're made of bone. An orchard of skeleton trees.

From the twisted boughs of what was once Bear, a black flower grows like a tumor. The petals snap open with a spew of feathers and from the gruesome womb, a crow fights his way free. He fixes his red gaze on me, screaming as he flaps his wings. I try to retreat from the macabre forest, but with every tentative step, a fresh bead of blood drips through my fingers, and new trees are born. The blood turns neon and slicks the trees. A high-pitched buzzing erupts in my ears.

I run, but the forest has fangs. The dead mouths of desert critters tear at my arms, serrating skin and spawning new scars: lilac spirals like the ones littering Crow's skin.

CROW

Blue eyes and blond hair. Wayne. He's gloating over me, his smile vicious and eyes dead-cold.

"Tell anyone and this'll go viral, squaw." Lilah leers at me.

I bide my time, enduring the shame, letting the rage and hatred build up inside of me while I pump serious iron, until one afternoon after practice, I find Wayne alone in the parking lot.

I'm not quite as tall as the running back but I'm just as strong, and he crumples when I kick his legs out from under him.

"Do you like that, dickhead?" I pummel his face, breaking everything I thought was beautiful about him. "Is this what you wanted?"

My fists connect with his skull and my whole body jolts, throwing me sideways into darkness.

Voices echo in the black as shadows flutter above me, coalescing into humanoid shapes.

"Again," someone says and another jolt rips through my body. It's like a giant hand reaches into my chest and squeezes my heart. Pain envelopes me, a liquid layer filling every pore.

```
tech1@cer-ro:~$ reboot
```

Scorching white light drips into my eyes and the fist in my chest releases its grip. I can breathe again. The high-pitched whine in my ear becomes a steady beeping.

"He's back," the voice says.

A familiar voice becomes distinct. **"Well that was**

unexpected," he says.

"**You didn't do this?**"

"**Nope. The algorithm was set to amp up fears. Guess there's a deeper emotional attachment here.**"

"**That shouldn't be possible.**"

"**Dude, this is unchartered territory. Everything is possible.**"

RALEIGH

Pacing up and down the waiting room doesn't make news of Crow—Brennan—come any quicker. I wish I knew who answered the call and what they said. Seems an awful coincidence he has some kind of fit right after dialing that number on the card. And what about the surgery I saw? Maybe I was right about cybertech or a brain implant. I rub the back of my neck, fingers searching for a scar I can't possibly have, yet it somehow wouldn't surprise me if I did.

"You all right?" Abi sips from a Styrofoam cup of decaf. There's no way I can tell her about having Brennan's memories, about our weird connection. She'll smile sadly and tell me I should see my shrink; she'll try to convince me being medicated isn't anything to be ashamed of and I might believe her.

"Just thinking about last time we were here." I force the words out. We were waiting on news of Weston. Guilt sinks its teeth into me. I should've insisted Brennan get checked out, should've dragged his ass to the ER that first night and consequences be damned.

"You'll wear a track if you keep that up." A woman stands with one hand on her jutting hip, the woman from the diner with the severe haircut. A man stands beside her in a dark suit, his expression unreadable.

"Who are you?" My words come out as brittle as shed snakeskin.

"Are you a doctor?" Abi asks, her gaze raking up and down the woman before giving me a furtive glance.

"Special Agent O'Driscoll," she says with a scowl. The floor opens up beneath me: a vortex of spiraling darkness. I've gone and done it now. It won't be county jail or juvie this time; it'll be Coyote Creek for life.

"You're FBI?" Abi slinks closer to me and takes my hand.

"Special division of Homeland Security." O'Driscoll flashes her badge—black and gold and pure intimidation. The man does the same without saying anything.

"Homeland Security." Abi gulps.

"That's not what you told my mother." And why would the DHS be worried about old ladies out in the desert?

"We are whoever we need to be. Your mother seemed delicate." Her accent is chic and cultured, the type cultivated in New England mansions. "Raleigh Alaska Williams, right?"

"Sounds like you already know."

"Mind if we talk in private?" Her gaze flicks to Abi.

"And if I do mind?" *Inhale*. Do not antagonize her. *Exhale*. Do not lose it. I don't trust her, no matter what badge she carries, and I know my rights.

"Then I can arrest you for obstruction, and we'll have this conversation at the local station with Sheriff Daniels."

"Raw, just do as she says." Abi detaches her fingers from mine and nudges me forward. "I'll wait here."

"Should I call my lawyer?" I ask.

"I doubt that's necessary." O'Driscoll gives me an ice-cold smile. "Long as you cooperate."

"This ain't my first rodeo." Reluctantly, I follow her down the corridor. The man falls in step behind me.

"I'm sure it isn't. And being familiar with the justice system, you'll know it's in your best interests not to piss me off." O'Driscoll fixes me with an atomic glare that gets me riled. No matter what badge they carry, cops are all the same.

"You gonna tell me how Crow is?" My heart hammers in my ears and cold sweat trickles down my spine.

"Who?"

"Um, Brennan Cozens?"

"Did he tell you his name?" She narrows her gaze, and I feel cornered.

"Just tell me how he is."

"He'll be fine." She gestures for me to enter the elevator and I comply, wary of the 9mm on her hip and the heat the other guy's packing.

"You were at the diner."

"You're sharp as a tack." O'Driscoll sends us to the lower levels.

"But if you've been looking for Brennan all this time, why wait until now to arrest him?"

"He's not under arrest." O'Driscoll doesn't say more and the elevator pings. The doors open on an underground lot. Two black SUVs are waiting, engines running and the other man from the diner stands beside an open passenger door.

"That him?" the man asks.

"It is," O'Driscoll answers. "Is the subject on board?"

Subject?

"Yes, sir," the man says.

"Let's go, Preston." O'Driscoll shoves me toward the vehicle, and a doctor wearing scrubs and a surgical mask emerges with a syringe in hand.

"What's happening? Where's Crow?" I hesitate.

"We're taking you in for questioning. Get in, kid." O'Driscoll's expression is harder than the lines on her suit. I've been in trouble with the law before. This isn't how they operate. Something's not right, and there's no way I'm getting into the SUV until I know what's cutting.

"I'm not going anywhere with you." I plant my feet and fold my arms. "I know my rights."

"We don't have time for this." O'Driscoll rolls her eyes and nods to the agent behind me. He steps closer but doesn't touch me, his hand resting on his gun.

"Get in," O'Driscoll orders.

"Am I under arrest?"

"Do you want to be?" She glowers.

"If I am, then I'll definitely be waiting for my lawyer, thanks."

"Grab him," O'Driscoll says. The man behind me grabs my elbow and slams me against the vehicle, twisting my arm behind my back.

"This is police brutality." I resist the urge to fight him. He's strong and he's got the gun and badge.

"I'll make this brutally simple for you, then." O'Driscoll steps up beside me as the doctor tugs up the sleeve of my T-shirt with gloved fingers. No way I'm letting him stick me with that.

"Hold him still." The doctor's breath is rough against my ear and brings back unwanted memories of the last time someone had me pinned down against my will. The man twists my wrist and pain weaves up my arm. The doctor sticks the needle in, but I jerk sideways and the syringe tears free, dropping to the floor.

"In twenty-nine days, you're hoping to take the MarsLife tests. We can help make your dreams come true," O'Driscoll says. "We can also shatter them."

"What are you talking about? Who are you?" My shoulder burns and I squirm in the guy's grip, bracing for a counter attack if he doesn't let me go.

There's a thwack followed by a grunt. Preston crumples beside the front wheel. Brennan brandishes a 9mm, barefoot and clad in only a hospital gown with cannula still attached to his face. Brain gunk crusts both ears and trails down his neck. Is he the "subject"?

"Let him go."

"You don't wanna do this, kid." O'Driscoll holds up her hands. The guy holding me jerks my arm up higher. He's going to dislocate my shoulder. I grit my teeth and wait, timing my move. The doctor scrambles backward and drops the syringe again, eyes wide with fright staring at Brennan.

"I will if I have to." The gun shakes in Brennan's hand. He must've pistol whipped Preston. The agent is sprawled out on the ground, unconscious, blood smearing his temple.

"You're sick. You need our help." O'Driscoll does something with her fingers and the man momentarily eases his weight off my back. I seize the moment and wrench free, driving my elbow into his stomach hard, following it up with a punch to his face. The scabs on my knuckles tear open and my finger joints scream in pain.

Brennan fires and misses by a mile.

"Stupid boy." O'Driscoll takes aim. Shots ring out, and I dive in front of Brennan. We crash to the floor, my temple smacking into concrete in my attempt to protect him. More shots, or are my ears still ringing from the first one? The fluorescent glare of the light above pulses and increases in intensity as if I'm staring at the sun. The world loses detail, washing out in smears of gray.

"We're going to put you under now. Count back from ten."

Ten...nine...my eyes close...seven...six...I won't be the same after this...four...three...

"Raleigh, can you hear me?" Brennan's face swims into focus. "Can you get up?" He hauls me to my feet. Liquid fire runs in molten bands around my head and pools above my left temple.

"Can you walk?" Brennan asks.

It hurts to talk, to move, to think, but I manage to nod.

"Let's go." He shuffles me into the car before getting behind the wheel. The car pulls off leaving three bodies in its wake and the doctor huddled beside the front wheel of the